Deep Down There

Deep Down There

By

Oli Jacobs

To the fine folk at Unbound for taking a chance, and giving me the belief

And, of course, to those that originally backed the book, reinforcing that belief

Also by Oli Jacobs

Bad Sandwich
The Children of Little Thwopping
The Station 17 Chronicles
Wilthaven

The Kirk Sandblaster series:

Kirk Sandblaster: Space Adventurer
Kirk Sandblaster and the Ice Pirates of Llurr
Kirk Sandblaster Plays the Game of Yloria
Kirk Sandblaster Faces TETRAGEDDON
Kirk Sandblaster vs. Montague Santiago
Kirk Sandblaster & Xlaar's World War
Kirk Sandblaster vs. Protocol 9
Kirk Sandblaster Faces the End

The Mr Blank series:

Wrapped Up in Nothing
Night Train

The Filmic Cuts series:

Sunshine and Lollipops
Luchador Monkey Crisis
Curse of the Ellipsis…
Title Pending
Suplex Sounds of the 70s
The Lament of the Silver Badger

Also featured in:

Flash Fear
Subject Verb Object

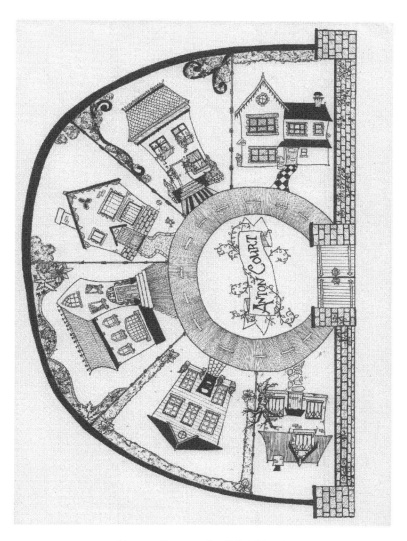

(Anton Court art by Eli Allison)

DAY 1

"What the bloody Hell is this?"

What the bloody Hell it was, was a hole.

Specifically, a perfectly round hole, about 6-feet wide, and so dark inside that it seemed to consume the light that dared try to illuminate it.

The most intriguing thing about it was that it wasn't in Anton Court the day before.

Where once were a host of lovely communal flowers, and a little patch of grass for the children to play upon, now sat this alien abyss. There were no chips to suggest it was dug, nor any tools to suggest who may have dug it.

It was just there, a perfect circle leading down into the ground.

A development that some of the Anton Court residents loudly did not care for.

The voice that had woken Hannah Suggs belonged to James Stanley, know by all as The Colonel due to his proud history in the military. This had evolved him into a blustery type, quick to let his feelings known about everything and anything whether anyone was listening or not. His wife, Heather, mostly stood by and hoped that The Colonel's temper didn't flare up too violently and cause another heart scare.

The recipient of this morning's rant was Anton Court's resident custodian Vincent Crendon. He was the go-to man to fix taps, trim hedges, and make sure your house was in tip-top condition. This was due to the fact that Anton Court was a gated community consisting of five houses, owned by the company HP Properties as somewhere for folk to live in relative peace. Crendon was in charge of maintaining this peace, housed in a small bungalow that sat at the end of the arched dwellings. So far, he had achieved this with relative ease.

Then, the hole appeared.

Considering the prices that HP Properties charged the residents for the opportunity to live in Anton Court, a sudden appearance of a dangerous hole could easily rankle. And sure enough, The Colonel was the man for the rankling.

"So, what the Hell are you going to do about it?"

Crendon looked down the hole, while other residents filtered out of their homes to see what the fuss was about. The first to make their presence known were Rich Davis and his girlfriend, Stacey Lloyd. Rich was one of these modern businessmen who had made their money in digital apps, although Hannah didn't know exactly *what* apps Rich had made, nor what they did. All she and the other residents knew was that he preferred gauchely coloured shirt and shorts to a suit, had the odd excessive party, and enjoyed various holidays and adventures with Stacey.

In the few times they had met, Hannah felt that Stacey had the personality of a paper bag. Which she considered slightly insulting to the bag.

A couple of houses down, she could see Tim and Louise Cooper watching from their front door, making sure to shield their daughter Samantha from any random outbursts of expletives from The Colonel. Like many of the households, the family had lived in Anton Court since it opened a few months previously, and Hannah found they were good company when she needed a respite from looking after her two sons, Jarelle and Warren.

Finally, joining her in her window-based voyeurism, were William and Charles Barrett, a middle-aged couple that were always keen to ingratiate themselves in the small community. Hannah couldn't help feel they were overcompensating at times, but enjoyed their company enough not to dwell on it too much. Besides, Charles was her partner in crime these days when it came to gossip, ideology, and Irish coffees. Noting her own nosing, he shot her a conspiratorial wink as they watched the show go on.

Then there was Hannah herself. It hadn't always been just the three of them, though. She had moved into Anton Court with her partner Greg six months ago.

Three months later, he was gone, and it was just her and the boys.

She made do, thanks to the assistance of Greg's employer making sure she was OK, and the rest of the community helped a lot. Despite the vast range of personalities and mentalities, they did all get along in their own way. The odd communal dinner helped, as well as the fact that nobody was really that anti-social.

With the exception of The Colonel.

But then again, even he was involved in the new bond they were all cultivating over the hole.

"Are you going to answer me?" The Colonel said. With each word, he moved closer to Crendon in some show of phallic superiority. Alas, this was tempered somewhat by Crendon's proximity to the hole itself.

"I'm thinking."

"What's to think about? A bloody great ditch has appeared in our garden!"

"Really?"

Crendon's sarcasm never sat well with The Colonel, and it took Heather's gentle touch to prevent the old man from throwing Crendon down the hole.

"You been digging, Crendy?" Rich said.

Crendon just shook his head; his eyes were firmly fixed toward the hole, even as he stood back to gather his thoughts. With this sudden diversion, his relatively relaxed approach to his work had suddenly become quite the albatross.

For, in Crendon's mind, an issue like this is both easy to solve, and yet also quite tricky due to all the variables that tended to arise. And one thing Vincent Crendon didn't like was variables.

"Leave it to me," Crendon said.

"What do you mean, 'leave'?" The Colonel said.

"I mean, leave it to me. I'll look into it."

"We're all looking into it," Rich said with a smile.

No one else joined him.

"I'll be honest," Tim said, walking from his front door in a hastily thrown-on dressing gown. "I'm not too happy either. I mean, it's not safe, is it? Our daughter could fall in."

"Or my boys."

Hannah had now made her presence known, choosing to lean out of her bedroom window rather than bless the residents with the sight of her in her pyjamas. Although the idea of giving The Colonel heart palpitations was amusing.

You could see the stress building on Crendon's face, which only got worse when Rich inspected the hole himself.

"Looks pretty deep."

"It looks like a bloody eyesore."

"I wonder what caused it..."

"What..." The Colonel began to splutter, before Heather thankfully persuaded him that a hearty breakfast might settle his nerves. His point made, he ignored the perceived sass from Rich, and followed her back indoors. As Heather led him back, William sensed the scene was safe enough to come and join the growing crowd.

"New look for the Court?" he said. A pen stood firmly in the corner of his mouth, a sign of his longing for his old pipe.

"Seems like it," Tim replied, making sure to supply a handshake to the new member of the inspection group.

Naturally, all the men of Anton Court were now intrigued to look into the hole. It was a primal behaviour that Hannah had seen many times before at the odd community gathering, and it was always amusing. Now, she had the absurd sight of Rich, Tim, and William all looking down this brand new pit, while Crendon paced nearby, talking on his mobile.

As for her, she had no interest in a big hole. She had two boys to feed, and they weren't getting any more patient.

Especially when they found out about Anton Court's latest attraction.

The rest of the day trundled along rather mundanely for Hannah.

Jarelle and Warren caught the bus to school, although not before having a cheeky peek down the hole. Crendon was yet to do anything about it, and the thought of seeing one of them jump down made Hannah's chest feel tight.

But once they were on the bus, she relaxed, enjoying a coffee with Charles that was enhanced with a whiskey twist, as per their little tradition. Neither of them worked, so the day was always one for catching up on various gossip and talks of the town. Hannah was lucky to have the fiscal support of Greg's employers, and Charles was a creative sort who always seemed to be living the life of a bohemian. Normally, the two would look over various news sites and social media, but today there was a more important subject du jour.

The hole.

"I wouldn't be shocked if it was vandals," Charles said.

"How would they get through the gate?"

"My dear, anyone could get through if they were inspired enough. Crendon isn't the fine gatekeeper he thinks he is."

The two were sat on Charles's front lawn, watching the site manager work away on solving the riddle of the hole. When his name was mentioned, he glanced their way, as if his ears had suddenly heated up several degrees.

Charles waved.

Crendon didn't wave back.

"I remember when William and I first moved into Anton. We had a little private soiree and, shall we say, some sorts weren't invited. Court Rules. But of course, William and I have our ways, and so with our own brand of ingenuity, *par-tay*!"

Hannah remembered the occasion well, as Greg himself had briefly attended and returned home more than a little squiffy. Still, as nice as it was to reminisce, she had bigger, deeper, things on her mind.

"But why dig a hole?"

"Why not? Kids these days seem to lack creativity."

"But... a hole?"

"Hannah, dear, a hole is a hole. It's quick, simple, and most of all, *irritating*."

As Charles said that, he nodded over to the Stanley residence. Sure enough, hidden behind the net curtains, were the watchful eyes of The Colonel.

Hannah just shrugged and sipped her coffee.

It was a nice buzz, enhanced by the warmth of the rising sun.

After an hour of chatter, the two of them watched as Crendon opened the gates and beckoned in a van. On the side were the words GEDNEY

MAINTENANCE, and in the driver's seat was the kind of man that you would expect in such a vehicle.

As Charles noted, the sort of man Crendon would know.

The two self-proclaimed Queens of the Court watched over as Crendon and the other man walked toward the hole, looked in, and did the usual tuts of the tongue and scratches of the head that workmen are wont to do. It was fine theatre, especially after a few of Charles's coffee, but it did lack a certain something from this distance.

So Hannah got up to investigate.

With Charles tittering behind.

"What's the word, Crendon?"

Crendon looked up at Hannah approaching with Charles lurking behind her, and smiled. She knew he had always had a thing for her, and since Greg had gone, that had intensified a little. She'd be lying if she said she didn't take advantage of it, and had even confided in Charles that the odd drunken temptation was there. But as it was she was a widow, and Crendon was a gentleman. Despite what some may have thought of him.

"The word is, we've got a big hole."

"Cheeky," Charles said. Hannah stifled her laughter.

"Yeah, whatever. Anyway, my mate Ronnie here thinks it might be a sinkhole. One of those things that pop up now and again."

"Pop up? How can a hole just pop up?" Hannah asked.

Crendon answered by pointing at the hole.

Charles, however, wasn't convinced by this theory.

"Looks a bit too… *neat*, to be a sinkhole."

"Since when were you the geologist?" Crendon said.

"Since I took the same class you did?"

Crendon laughed. Of all the people who could keep up with his style of banter, Charles was the best. After a few drinks, it was fun to watch.

"I'm getting Ron to fetch some cement. We'll fill it up later today and that should sort it out."

"And in the meantime?" Hannah said.

"In the meantime, don't fall in."

It was fair advice. Even standing a few feet from it, Hannah felt a bit wobbly.

Although that could have been the coffee.

Talking of which, she needed another one. Sans the emerald spirit, of course.

After all, the kids would be home in a couple of hours.

By the time the cement truck arrived, the residents of Anton Court were back in their respective homes.

Most of them didn't have the time to watch a hole being filled with concrete, but those who were of a nosy persuasion were still snatching the occasional glances at the goings on. It wasn't every day that something exciting happened in their little community, and both Jarelle and Warren had been captivated by the scene since coming home. Hannah had watched them bounce by the windows, desperate to get a closer look, in between secretive mutterings. The situation had certainly sparked their imagination in such a short time.

The most impressive thing about the truck had been its size. Evidently, Crendon had decided to go hard on this crater, and given the amount of concrete the mixer held, he wasn't doing anything by half. While Crendon was having the usual workman's back-and-forth banter with Ronnie - the man behind the wheel – he was also responsible for fielding calls over what looked like more serious matters. As Hannah watched on, she saw Crendon gesticulate in defence, looking back at Ronnie as he prepared the truck. Each time the conversation ended and Crendon thought he was safe, another call would come through and his demeanour slumped.

Eventually, it was time for the truck's contents to go into the hole, and everyone in Anton Court was now watching. It was like Charles had said to Hannah once:

Everybody loves a show.

The cement poured quicker than Hannah expected, and the coos of awe from her boys made her laugh. The truck's contents came out in a steady, grey stream, thick like gravy and going directly into the centre of the hole. At first, Crendon looked pleased with his plan, watching as more and more liquid concrete fell into the pit. However, as the mixer tilted more and more, his pleasure turned to confusion, as he kept looking at the vehicle, and looking down the hole.

Despite emptying enough concrete to cover most of the Court in a thick lining, it had barely made a dent in the hole. Crendon was left looking down there, wondering how deep it went, while Ronnie concentrated on scratching his head.

Throughout the evening, Ronnie left, came back, and poured more concrete in the hole. Hour after hour, he attempted to fill it as Crendon watched, and each time neither man could understand why it wasn't close to being filled.

As the sun began to set, and the price of concrete began to hit figures that even HP Properties would baulk at, Crendon looked angrily at his new problem, and told Ronnie to come back tomorrow. In the meantime, he grabbed some panels from his home, hammered them strategically around the hole, and scrawled a sign on some paper -

Hannah laughed. As if they were going anywhere near it.

Although it certainly was tempting to have a look inside.

It was around 2:30 AM when the first rumble happened.

Of course, it was so innocuous, that nobody in Anton Court really noticed it. They were either snoring their slow drones into the night, or mumbling bizarre non-sequiturs based on dreams they'd soon forget.

No, they did not notice the rumble.

They noticed the first chunk of concrete, though.

Hannah woke up with a start thanks to the disquieting alarm of her screaming children. Acting purely on instinct, she rushed to Jarelle and Warren's room to find the two boys looking out the window. There, she saw what had caused their concern - a large chunk of hardened cement that had shattered their fence.

And more were coming.

Blasted from the hole.

As more of the residents woke up to this unusual assault, the more concrete was spewed forth from their brand new feature. Some chunks tumbled harmlessly around the road, while others flew several feet in the air, landing perfectly onto freshly mown lawns and carefully arranged flowerbeds.

At one point, The Colonel erupted from his front door. Hannah wasn't sure what was in his hand, but she knew she didn't want to find out.

Nobody would anyway, as Heather soon pulled him back in from the bombardment of mortar that struck their front path.

The idea of their homes being a safe place from the geyser of cement did not last long, as soon enough the volley of cement became more frequent and more violent. Chunks were thrown with obscene speed from the hole, flying in the air and striking the rooftops of Anton Court. Some harmlessly tumbled down, but Hannah watched as one sizable chunk punched a hole in the Barrett's home.

Just as quickly as the panic set in, however, the bizarre assault was over and the Court was quiet once more. Holding tight to her sons, Hannah watched as Crendon crept out of his bungalow, eyes wide and jaw hanging loose in a stunned silence. He looked over the chaos of what had just happened, shook his head, and drank from the bottle in his hand.

Whatever was in the hole, did *not* want to be covered.

DAY 2

There was a lot of shouting the next morning, mainly from The Colonel.

Due to his seniority in age, he believed in moments like these that he was the voice of the residents in Anton Court. Every spit of rage and lash of vitriol was said in the firm confidence that he spoke for everyone, whether they liked it or not. In truth, most of the time the others didn't care about a misshapen divot or a torn piece of mail, but when it came to an early morning storm of cement raining down upon their homes…

Crendon was well experienced in handling The Colonel. While the old man ranted and raved and made use of every curse word he knew, the caretaker simply carried on with his work, placing the chunks of concrete in one big pile near the front gate. Luckily, none were big enough to cause serious issue – save for the Barrett's roof – and even the largest stone was more cumbersome than heavy.

It was also made easier by the helping hand of Hannah, who thought it better to do some good in the community rather than sap away the daytime hours in a whiskey-soaked stupor with Charles. Armed with a pair of gloves and one of Greg's old shirts, she had carried huge shards of concrete from both her garden and her attic, where one or two lumps had managed to perforate her roof. Besides, much like the rest of Anton Court, she was as calm in the face of these damages as she was under the belief that HP Properties would cover it all.

What she, nor anyone else, knew was that HP Properties were very unhappy with Crendon and his concrete plan, and it was more likely that Crendon himself would be assigned the price of the clean up.

As the rubble thinned out around the curved road of the gated community, more folk came out to help. Both William and Rich had taken a day off from their respective schedules to help sweep and apply temporary solutions to broken buildings, and even Tim joined them for a while before an urgent call had taken him away. Hannah had actually been glad of this, as Tim wasn't one who was comfortable with getting his hands dirty, and was always nervous around The Colonel.

Especially when the old man was on the warpath.

She couldn't help but watch as the stress of The Colonel's bluster in one ear and the scolding of his bosses in the other was pulverising Crendon. As The Colonel launched into his latest vitriolic verse, and another mobile call was trying to be ignored, the caretaker finally broke.

"What do you think I'm going to do about it? What do you think I *am* doing about it? You have a problem? Talk to the management. You have a problem with me? Talk to the management. You have a problem living here? Move. The fuck. Out."

There was an eerie silence as The Colonel took these words on board, puffed violently through his nose, twisted his face, and turned back into his home. Heather – who had been taking the time to catch up with Tim's wife, Louise – ended their conversation and followed him inside.

They all knew that if anyone could calm The Colonel down, it was his wife.

"He's going to have a heart attack, one of these days," William said.

"If we're lucky," Rich said.

It wasn't that people hated The Colonel, it was just that he was hard to love. The few times Hannah had spoken to Heather, she was surprised by the difference in demeanour behind-the-scenes. Apparently, all the bluster and rage was only when he was outside his comfort zone. While most of the community in Anton Court made the effort to bond, The Colonel was always wary of such things.

"He just… lacks trust," Heather had told her, and they had left it at that.

"Maybe we can get him involved with the clean-up," Rich said. "Speed up the process."

Hannah ignored what he said and carried on shovelling the last bits of concrete. Rich always had a hard-on for poking The Colonel's temper, and doing so now would be a very bad idea.

Besides, it wasn't as if he was hard at work at that point. Rich was more interested in the hole itself than the contents it had purged. He'd move stuff about, but then take a moment to peek down into the crater for a long while.

For some reason, this irritated Hannah.

"What's so interesting?" she said.

"Oh, what? Nothing. Just..."

Rich seemed entranced by the hole. If Hannah was honest, so was she. Everyone was. Ever since it had appeared it had become the thing they thought about the most, but there was something more tugging at Rich's curiosity; Something that had hooked itself in and wasn't letting go.

"You ever just wanted to go on an adventure?" he said with a smile.

"Not really."

"I'm just thinking, what could have caused that? Last night?"

"A build up of gas?" William said. "If we consider this hole is deeper than we think, then it may have been caused by a deposit of natural resources."

Rich didn't seem so sure.

"Must have been a lot of gas," he said.

"Gas or not, can we just clean this up? The quicker we do that, the sooner I can catch up on the sleep I lost last night."

"Han, if you want to sleep, go for it," Rich said. "This is manly work after all..."

Hannah wanted to push Rich down the hole for that comment.

Then again, that was probably what he wanted.

They carried on picking up the pieces of Crendon's failed attempt to solve the hole problem for another couple of hours, until Ronnie returned with his truck and took all the debris away. While he was at Anton Court, he engaged with Crendon more intensely toward the hole.

As the Court custodian walked away from the departing truck, his resident assistants looked on.

"So what now?" William said.

Crendon fell silent and smiled toward them.

"Oh don't worry. I've got a plan."

While Crendon's plans were underway, the rest of Anton Court mused over the events of last night.

There was general agreement that whatever caused the rubble to start flying was whatever caused the hole in the first place. William once again gave his theory that it could have been caused by a build-up of natural gases, positing that he read that various pockets of such were erupting across the globe at random points, leading to similar holes appearing. However, this theory was swiftly dismissed due to the peculiar fact that the hole was perfectly carved into the ground.

"If it was made by a puff of air, why's it so smooth?" Rich said. "Surely you'd see some damage to the sides if it had collapsed or something?"

Rich had slowly made himself the main expert on the hole, despite a lack of any geological or archaeological expertise that the likes of someone like William Barrett had. Still, he spoke with enough confidence and swagger that you couldn't help feel yourself being led by his opinions. Hannah thought to herself this was probably how he became so successful.

She also couldn't help but agree with him. When she had looked down the pit, she had been intrigued by how neat the hole was. The walls were smooth, the edge was perfectly cut into the ground, and despite the recent vomit of cement, there was no debris around it at all. It reminded Hannah of something like an ice-cream scoop, one that had been pushed into the ground, twisted, and taken the earth with it leaving an unblighted shape.

The structural integrity of the hole wasn't the main question though. What everyone had found themselves thinking since its discovery was how deep was it? A few stones and small chunks of the failed concrete had been thrown in to test, but there had been no sound nor any indication of a landing. In addition, the sheer volume of wet cement that had been poured down there meant that it had to be deeper than 3 full, large tankers.

It was this idea that made the likes of Hannah and the Coopers nervous, due to the increasing curiosity of their kids.

Before any further query could continue, the gates of Anton Court opened once more for Ronnie Gedney and his cavalcade of tools. Instead of more cement, though, he was transporting a rather large sheet of metal. The residents watched on with interest as Crendon helped him remove it from his truck, place it over the hole, and drill it in place with many strategically placed rivets. Once done, Crendon stood back with Ronnie and smiled. It wasn't the prettiest addition to the Court's communal garden, but it would certainly fulfil its main intention.

Cover the hole.

"Let's see your natural gas throw that up," Crendon said, looking quite satisfied with his work. So satisfied, in fact, that he walked over the sheet and gave a few stamps of his foot for good measure.

While Crendon seemed pleased with this solution, there was an unspoken state of disturbance between the watching residents. Hannah, for one, didn't see the sheet of metal as a permanent solution, and wondered how long it would be before something happened to it. Then, there was the thought toward Crendon's methods, and whether either the local council or HP Properties approved. And judging by the calls he was getting, the latter did not.

But she shook off these thoughts, putting them down to an overactive imagination. She had a lot of time on her hands these days, and an inactive mind was a playground for such thoughts. In the end, there was really only one thing left to do.

Go inside, have a quick drink, and wait for the boys to come home.

The rest of the day in Anton Court went ahead as it normally did.

Kids returned from school, residents returned from work, and The Colonel watched as Crendon and his crew of labourers went about fixing the damage of the previous night. It was as if by placing a simple sheet of metal over the hole, the problem it caused had now gone away.

Or so everyone thought.

Hannah couldn't help but notice that nagging feeling in her head was getting worse. She couldn't describe it, but it had begun around the time that Greg had passed away. Since the hole had appeared, it intensified from an ill feeling to a throbbing migraine. More a sickness of the soul than of the mind. It wasn't unbearable, but it was like an itch that was just out of reach, constantly sizzling away.

It wasn't helped by her boys asking about the hole. Kids are inquisitive, Hannah knew that, but their interest in a simple crater bordered on the obsessive.

"Where do you think it came from?" Jarelle said.

"Who did it?" Warren said.

And the one that nagged at her the most.

"What's down there?" they both had said.

Many times.

Like many parents before her, she entertained their curiosity for a little bit, but it had soon gotten to the stage that, combined with her growing migraine, the best she could offer was a patient smile hiding gritted teeth.

They weren't the only ones that the hole entranced. Samantha, Tim and Louise's little one, also found herself pausing by the metal sheet that now covered the pit. Despite the beckoning from her parents, Hannah watched as Samantha stood there for a long time, just looking at where the hole used to be.

When Jarelle and Warren asked if they could go too, that was when Hannah brought out her secret weapon.

Ice cream.

Children were very predictable like that.

As the night drew in and the boys were settled in their beds, Hannah debated the merits of going over and catching up on the gossip with Charles. Instead, she just sat by the window and watched Anton Court become enveloped by darkness. The street lamps lit up on cue, and she could now see that the only evidence of the eruption the night before were a few crushed flowers and some dents in the road.

But Hannah found it wasn't the damage that she was interested in, it was the hole.

And she wasn't the only one.

From where she sat, she could see across to Rich and Stacey's place, where the wannabe adventurer looked at the hole himself. Stacey was muttering something behind him, but nothing was distracting Rich from his focus. Hannah couldn't help but feel that, should Crendon let him, Rich would be the first down the hole.

But it was covered with metal now and no longer an issue.

Until the early hours came round once more.

As the lights in the homes of Anton Court went out, and the only sound was the light wash of wind within the small cul-de-sac, nothing really happened. Which was par for the course for areas such as these. One of the appealing aspects of the Court was that it was in a quiet area surrounded by fields, away from the hustle and bustle of most parts of suburbia. They weren't isolated, but they were blessed without the pox of busy roads and active environments.

Then, the hole had appeared.

At first, there was nothing to suggest anything out of the ordinary was about to occur. The stillness within the Court drifted happily from house to house.

Then, the first *CLASH* happened.

In truth, there may have been many more before that, but this was the one that got the attention of Hannah and the other residents. It was a smashing against steel that was loud enough to echo through Anton Court, and followed by a rumble that was as unsettling as it was the previous night.

Then came the next *CLASH*, louder than the previous one.

Without a second thought, all the residents headed toward their windows and looked out. All watching the same thing.

The hole.

As they all watched, they saw how, in the dim light of the early hours, the sheet of metal over the hole had now been dented. From the bottom. Instead of a sheet, it now resembled a tiny hill straining to stay attached to where Crendon had drilled it in.

Not that it was staying like that, as another *CLASH* sent the buckled sheet flying into the air, landing perfectly in William and Charles's garden.

There would be much discussion the next day over what happened then, but the thing most residents, including Hannah, would not admit to was what they saw from within the hole. Whatever had caused the reinforced sheet to be punched away, it wasn't gas as William suggested. In fact, you would even question if it were 'natural' at all.

Hannah wasn't sure what it was, but she knew that she saw something retreat back down the hole, safe in its deep darkness.

DAY 3

There was a sense of unease around the Court the next day.

Usually, Friday would instigate a feeling of excitement over the pending weekend, but now there was only a fear over what had happened the previous night.

Still sat battered in William and Charles's garden was the steel sheet Crendon had used to try and cover the hole. While the plan was solid enough – as was the sheet used – it now lay upside down several metres away from the crater, resembling a bowl rather than a panel.

This time, there was no uproar from any of the residents. There were no questions or queries, just a stunned silence over what had happened. Many had also seen what Hannah believed she had seen, but did not want to come across as the crazy one who would broach the subject. Therefore, the only option was to look at what happened in stunned silence, and continue on with their day.

And so those that had day jobs went to work, and those who were blessed with children sent them to school. All attempts at normality were put into action.

For those who enjoyed the home life – including Hannah, Charles, and Rich and Stacey – they had decided to join Crendon in the inspection of the dented metal. As for The Colonel and Heather, they remained indoors, with The Colonel only occasionally scouting for developments.

As they all took in the sight of the shunted steel, Rich finally broke the tense silence.

"So?"

"So William's hydrangeas aren't going to recover," Charles said.

"I was talking about the cover."

"You don't say."

Crendon didn't say anything. He just got on his phone and muttered to Ronnie in a trance. Everyone else set about sharing their thoughts on what happened.

"I don't like it," Stacey said.

"Eh?"

"It's weird."

"It's not weird, it's…"

"Weird," Hannah said.

"It's an eyesore, that's what it is, my dear."

"Not something for your collection then, Charlie?"

"It's Charles, Richard, and no. I don't think this would sell."

Crendon came back and began by apologising to Charles about his garden, and then assured those left that the damage would be sorted out. Still noticeable by their absence were both HP Properties and the local council, but Crendon remained determined to keep everything under control and stammered out a declaration of returning everything to normal.

Of course, such a statement soon turned around to bite him.

"How's a hole in the middle of the Court normal?" Hannah said.

Crendon just glared. "It's being sorted."

"It's been sorted twice," Charles said.

"Yeah, well, it'll be sorted again. Besides, how do I know this isn't your work? Like, some sort of installation thing."

"My dear Vincent, I'm a collector. A curator. *Not* a creator."

Crendon sneered. "Yeah, well if I find out this is a joke, from any of you, your tenancy is revoked, alright?"

Nobody said anything. They all knew that Crendon didn't believe his own accusation, nor did he really have the power to evict them. But he was getting frustrated, and that bred a certain type of tenacity. If it were up to him, he'd write the whole mess off.

The problem was that the mess was a 6-feet wide hole.

And options were fast running out.

Once again, Ronnie appeared in Anton Court.

And once again, the residents of Anton Court watched as he went into conference with Crendon. They both performed the well-practiced workman's routine of looking, tutting, thinking, and ultimately shaking their heads in consternation.

As Hannah watched this show alongside Charles, the two of them sipped their drinks and provided their own acerbic commentary.

"Fancy thinking this was an installation," Charles said, his sneer almost twisting off his face. "Like I'd ever be involved in something so cheap."

"Plus you'd need to have the ability to dig a hole."

"Cheek. I'll let you know I'm quite the handyman."

"So I've heard," Hannah said, smiling into her drink.

Before Charles could prepare his latest retort, Stacey appeared from her home with Rich, eager to join in the fun with her two new 'gal pals'. She had disappeared with Rich earlier for reasons that Charles could only speculate, and Hannah could only assume. Suffice to say, her new rugged hairstyle was a strong indicator of such matters.

"So what's happening?" she said, with only the slightest desperation at being part of the so-called 'cool' crowd.

"There's a hole, Stacey," Charles said. "Same as always."

Crendon and Ronnie were finished looking over the hole, and were now investigating the sheet of metal that had been dragged from William and Charles's garden to the road. While it was no longer an eyesore within Charles's flora, the soil-stained groove in his grass wasn't much better.

"Figured it out yet?" Hannah shouted over to Crendon. The site manager just looked up, gave the briefest and fakest smile she'd ever seen, and went back to investigating the geographical intruder.

This was all entertaining, of course, but it was really a bigger distraction from the elephant in the room; nobody yet could figure out what had caused the panel to be punched away from the hole, and nobody would admit that they saw anything do so. Much like Hannah, they definitely did see *something*, but the idea of what they *think* they saw was so unpleasant it was easier to forget.

Something that was being made easier by Charles's brand of coffee.

"Ooh," he said, giving Hannah a nudge. "Now the real fun will begin."

The 'real fun' came in the form of The Colonel, who had watched on long enough and was now ready to have his say again. He marched on over to where Crendon and Ronnie stood, looking over the indent of the panel, and once he was in speaking distance, let rip.

"So how do you explain this?"

"It's under control, Mr Stanley."

"So you say, Crendon, but it doesn't look like it's under control, does it?"

As Crendon did his best to smile at The Colonel, Ronnie took a closer look at the panel.

"If you have any complaints, you know who to address them to."

"Oh, so HP Properties know about this, do they?"

Crendon screwed his face up at this, knowing that while they did, they were very unhappy about it.

"What about the council, Crendon? Are they privy to our latest feature?"

Ronnie noticed on the panel was a layer of rust, right in the epicentre of the indentation. It was a dark burgundy colouring, and splattered lightly across the metal.

"Perhaps even the police should be notified?"

The mention of the police really jarred Crendon. It was bad enough he had gone against HP Properties specific orders to leave the hole alone, it would be worse if the police managed to gain entry to Anton Court. For reasons best known to themselves, HP weren't keen on having an official present in their gated community.

Before any further stress could violate Crendon even further, Ronnie began screaming various colourful words.

This was after the hired handyman had swiped his finger over what he thought was rust, looked at it as it stained his finger, and continued to watch as his skin started to bubble and a burning pain began to take hold.

It was hard not to bear witness to Ronnie's decaying digit. He stood there, roaring in agony, as he held the tainted finger before him for all to see. The flesh had begun to turn a dark red and weep blood, causing it to pour past the knuckle and in steady streams down Ronnie's arm. The more he shook, everyone noted how the skin sloped off the bone, revealing sinew that was barely holding the finger together.

As Ronnie collapsed to the ground, and both Crendon and The Colonel ceased their debate to gawp in bewilderment, Hannah decided to take some sort of action and help the poor man. With a mug half-full of booze-infused coffee, she threw the contents toward Ronnie's hand and doused the disintegrating finger.

They all looked on, stunned in place by what they just witnessed, while Ronnie coiled up on the floor and sobbed in pain.

As the ambulance took Ronnie away, the residents of Anton Court stood looking at the sheet of metal that had caused the horrific injuries to his finger. The paramedics who looked at it compared it to a chemical burn, with the skin eventually eroding right to the bone, and barely stopping at the knuckle. Thanks to Hannah's quick thinking, the tradesman would only lose a finger rather than his whole hand.

The incident was quickly swept under the proverbial carpet as, due to the drama Ronnie's injuries caused, Crendon had to make a call to HP Properties. Almost immediately, two suited officials showed up at Anton Court and made great efforts to talk to Ronnie and accompany him to the hospital.

No doubt armed with all sorts of compensation.

Such offers would not sway the likes of The Colonel, though, as the presence of the hole and what it could contain were now becoming a bigger headache than anyone could imagine. The sheet of metal that attempted to cover it could easily be disposed of, but it was becoming clear that they could not simply cover up a problem of this magnitude.

Not only that, but the presence of Anton Court's owners also put some pep in the old man's bluster.

Unfortunately for him, such a conference with HP Properties' current representative was denied, as the suited man instead ignored The Colonel's request for a quick word in order to speak privately with Crendon. Not to be shunned, The Colonel opted to announce his 'Plan B'.

"I'm calling the council right now," The Colonel said.

This caught the attention of both Crendon and the HP Properties man. They both stopped their saunter to Crendon's bungalow and turned to face The Colonel.

"I wouldn't recommend that," Crendon said.

"Why ever not? Surely they'd be able to sort this out?" Charles said.

"Just… bear with me one moment."

As Crendon spoke, the residents caught the look on the HP Properties man. It was cold and vaguely threatening, the kind that you'd give a naughty child as a warning. But while that would usually lack intent, there was nothing innocent about this look.

As Crendon was escorted to his bungalow, the remaining residents 'stood in stunned awe at what had happened. Instead of going back to their usual lives, they just lingered in a fugue state, staggered by how things had escalated in the past couple of days.

Hannah was especially groggy. She thought it was the mix of coffee and the interrupted sleep of the past nights, but there was something else about it. She felt like she was hallucinating, and without knowing, found herself nearing the precipice of the hole, where a familiar voice seemed to be calling her.

"… need to act."

The comment had been low, under a hushed tongue, but it was enough to break Hannah from her stupor. Which was a good thing, as she was closer to the hole than she would have liked. Shaking herself back to reality, she turned to who had said the words and saw The Colonel speaking to Charles. Usually, the two would be engaged in some sort of bitter diatribe, but curiously they seemed rather civil for once.

When Charles noticed Hannah watching them, he smiled broadly.

"Colonel is just telling me all about his plans to get the council involved."

As Charles spoke, The Colonel noted Hannah's attention and added his trademark scowl to his features. "It's a bloody disgrace."

Hannah just nodded. She was still feeling the effects of her brief moment of lost lucidity.

As Charles came over and casually pulled her away from the hole, Hannah couldn't help but look back at it. No matter how absurd it seemed, she had been absolutely certain she had heard Greg's voice down there.

Maybe she just needed a nap.

Within the hour, every resident of Anton Court got an email. It was addressed from HP Properties, and came with a fancy letterhead and bold text to get your attention. It read:

Dear Resident

We understand that recent events have left you feeling uneasy about your tenancy here at Anton Court. For that, we can only apologise. HP Properties pride themselves on creating communities where select people can come together in safety and comfort, away from the bustle of everyday life. Of course, the mere fact you are receiving this message shows how valued you are as a resident here at Anton Court.

Site Manager Vincent Crendon has given us all the information regarding the recent incident involving a sinkhole appearing overnight within the Court's communal garden, and also the failed attempts to solve this issue. For that, we can only apologise once more. Mr Crendon was hired for his expertise in such matters, and we have absolute faith in his skills moving forward.

Of course, he has also informed us that you are looking to obtain an exterior solution to this problem. For this, HP Properties completely understands your concerns and wishes. However, due to the nature of our business, we look to work independently from any council authority where possible. This is so we can continue to evolve our reputation as a safe, comfortable community building business.

In light of these events, HP Properties is willing to offer you, our trusting residents, compensation in the form of 6 months waived payment of tenancy fees, and also accommodation at the 5-star Garry Hotel, fully paid for by HP Properties (including meals, use of facilities, and other amenities) over the duration of solving this problem.

Once again, HP Properties thanks you for your patience in this matter. We are aware of how unique, and troublesome, such an event can be on your overall quality of life here in Anton Court, but we are dedicated to provide the utmost duty of care to make sure that your tenancy here is indeed a pleasant one.

Thank you for your patience, and we look forward to hearing from you.

William Dyer

Community Manager, HP Properties

"It's a tempting offer."

This was an understatement to say the least. Hannah was round Tim and Louise's house, watching the kids play together while they discussed the ins and outs of the HP Properties letter. In terms of compensation, it was one hell of a deal – free board at a 5 star hotel as well as 6 months free living? It was almost too good to be true, something William Barrett couldn't help but note.

Charles was more curious about the potential amenities.

For now, however, the Barretts were staying put. Or, at least, William was. The hole had tickled his scientific curiosity and to simply leave it be felt like a wasted opportunity.

The Coopers weren't too sure.

"I mean, it would be a nice break," Louise said. "But I can't help but think that by doing that, we…"

"Give up our right to complain?" Hannah said.

"Well it doesn't say that anywhere in the letter," Tim said. He'd been analysing it ever since the residents had received the email. "So, legally, it isn't an admission of acceptance over current circumstances."

"I think it's implied though."

"Maybe. It *is* a tempting offer…"

Hannah wasn't so easily swung. She had struggled to ingratiate herself since Greg had gone, and wasn't willing to give up her home due to a hole in the ground. Already, HP Properties had questioned whether she'd be able to keep up her 'status' here in Anton Court.

She had shown them exactly what that 'status' was, in not so many words.

All of them were not fit for the ears of her sons.

There was the small matter of the kids, though. Hannah did wonder whether it was a safe environment to be in, especially as Crendon had seemingly given up all attempts to place a fence around the hole. For now, it was just left there, gaping in the middle of the grass.

Not only that, there was something else about it. Something she had noticed the other day.

It was getting bigger.

"Well, I know Rich isn't taking the offer," Tim said. "The whole thing seems to excite him."

"No wonder. He's like a teenager, that man."

This was true. Rich had been coveting the hole since it appeared. Every day, he had been gazing down into it, thinking over what was down there, and literally itching to have a look. For now, Crendon's attempts to cover it had prevented him from pursuing anything seriously.

Now, there was no such barrier.

Literally.

"I could take up the offer, with the kids, while you stay here?" Louise said. "That wouldn't be an admission of acceptance over... it."

For some reason, nobody could address the hole simply as it was. It became something more than a crater. It was *something* other than that, they just didn't know *what*.

"I'm not going," Hannah said, finishing her drink. "But the kids..."

She looked around, and didn't immediately see Jarelle or Warren.

And neither Tim nor Louise could see Samantha.

The adult fear soon kicked in, as the parents realised they had been so distracted with HP Properties' incredible offer, they had let the kids wander off. As they all jumped from their seats in panic and began searching frantically, it wasn't until a shout from Crendon alerted them to their presence.

The three children were near the hole.

Armed with large amounts of food.

Hannah was the first out the door, watching as Warren froze in Crendon's sights. Jarelle turned around and immediately knew he was in trouble, backing away from the pit and putting his hands up as if to say 'nothing to do with me'. As for Samantha, she was happy throwing uncooked rashers of bacon down the hole, without a care in the world.

"What are they doing?" Crendon said, now seeing both Hannah and the Coopers appear from their house.

Of course, Hannah didn't have an answer, just heading toward Warren while Jarelle denied all knowledge about the whole enterprise. With a quick glare, she turned toward Warren and picked him up, the tears already dripping down his cheeks. Her sons had never really had to deal with adult anger on the level of Crendon, and the site manager wasn't exactly soft in his approach.

Not that he could understand what the children were doing anyway. As Tim scooped up Samantha, she was still tossing slices of chicken down the hole. Both sets of parents tried stern words, but everyone was just trying to figure out the whys, rather than fixate on the very real danger of them falling in.

After a moment of relief that they were a safe distance, Hannah finally got her sons in front of her and asked the important question.

"What were you doing?"

"Sam… Samantha said that we needed to feed it," Warren said.

"Feed what?"

The boy just shrugged. When Hannah turned to Jarelle, he joined in.

When Hannah would speak to Louise later, she would clarify what Samantha had said to her. Apparently, during the night, 'something' had grumbled, and Samantha decided that whatever was making the noise, was obviously hungry.

Hannah was just concerned over *what* was making 'the noise'.

Mostly, because she had heard it too.

Given her fears regarding HP Properties and their feelings toward her tenancy, it was a relief to have a visit from Perry.

She was the person hired by Greg's employers to make sure Hannah was OK and handling the loss of her partner. Perry wasn't a psychiatrist, per se, but was someone who had a very special skill in dealing with people. Plus, she could allay any paranoia Hannah had regarding the letter HP Properties sent, and whether they could finally evict her.

"Not without going through us," Perry said.

"You seem pretty sure," Hannah said, pouring Perry a cup of coffee free of Charles's Celtic spirit.

"Absolutely sure, Miss Suggs. Greg was a key employee at our company and his residence here was something that was imperative to his job. Therefore, legally, any issues regarding tenancy would be addressed to us, not to him or even yourself."

Hannah didn't quite understand this, nor did she understand Greg's work. She had never been given the name of his company, or a complete understanding of what they did. Greg claimed it was "mostly research", but research didn't explain why he was in a car accident during a trip to the Scottish Islands.

"Miss Suggs, you don't need to worry," Perry said, offering a comforting hand.

"That's easy for you to say. You don't live here."

"Of course not. But we understand business. And we understand what a home means to someone such as yourself. That said, maybe this offer…"

"I'm not leaving," Hannah said, her words as firm as her glare.

Perry just nodded slowly. "I understand."

"I can't leave. Then they'd win. You know?"

Again, Perry just nodded.

"I just…"

Before any more words came, the tears beat them to it. They weren't heavy sobs; just the small kind that leaks out when one cannot repress their emotions anymore.

"I remind you, Hannah, that if you have any problems, anything at all, we are here to help."

Hannah looked at Perry, barely convinced by the woman's warm smile.

"And who is 'we' exactly?"

Perry rolled her answer around in her head.

"Your friends," she said, continuing to placate Hannah with a warm, well-practiced smile.

It was a restless night.

Hannah had put the boys to bed, making sure to punish them fairly for going near the hole. She hated discipline if she was honest, but she knew how it would be seen if her sons were seen to be unruly. Being a single mother was bad enough. Being the single mother of two non-white boys? They may as well be in a gang.

For now, they were in bed, and that was good enough for Hannah.

She couldn't as easily go to sleep. Instead, she thought over what the children had said, and watched dumbly as Crendon went about attempting to construct a fence. He applied some posts, some wire, but eventually just dropped his tools to the floor and visibly sighed. He knew it was a fools errand - no matter what kind of barrier he put, he didn't have the ability to make something like this kid-proof.

So in the end, he gave up and left it.

And so the hole remained open that night, its maw wide to breathe in the night air.

Hannah couldn't shake the feeling that it was definitely becoming more than just an eyesore. There was a vibe around it, an aura that seeped inside your pores and didn't let go. It was ridiculous, of course; it was just a hole in the ground. And yet, she couldn't help but *feel* something about it.

No matter what she did around the house, Hannah couldn't distract herself from it. Whether she watched some TV or drank a glass or several of wine, she still knew the hole was there, still gaping and… inviting. It seemed to lure, to beckon one to delve inside, be devoured like the light that died within its ominous black.

It got worse when she went to bed.

It felt like she was awake all night, but there were several little things that contested that idea. The first was that she distinctly remembered the odd shudder in her bed, and turning to see the numbers on her digital clock bounce around and change.

The second was that she got up.

And that she went outside toward the hole.

She tried telling herself it was just a dream. That's all. It wasn't real despite all her senses screaming at her otherwise. She was still in bed. Safe in bed.

Not standing before the hole.

Where she heard him again.

Greg.

"Hay-bay…"

It was a nickname she hadn't heard in a long time. Or, at least, it felt like a long time.

It felt like forever.

"Hannah? Hay-bay? You there?"

Hannah felt herself shiver in the cold night air. She was paralysed to the spot, arms by her side, eyes fixed on only one thing.

The hole.

"Hay-bay?"

She was in her bed. This wasn't real. This wasn't happening. It was just a dream.

A nightmare.

"Hannah?"

It was like a trance, a paralysing hypnosis that wouldn't let go. Hannah felt her face become wet with the tears conjured by Greg's voice. He sounded so chipper, so real.

But he wasn't.

Was he?

"Come on, stop playing around. Where are you?"

Hannah wanted to call back, but every part of her body was locked in place. Now she was here before the hole, her role was that of spectator. An audience for the hole to show her what it had, what it could give her if only she embraced it.

"Hannah?"

Suddenly, she moved. One foot forward, the other following suit.

Until she was on the edge of the hole, looking down.

"Hey, Hay-bay!"

There was Greg.

But it wasn't. It couldn't be.

It was something that looked like Greg. Almost exactly. But…

"Are you coming?"

It wasn't him.

It was a horrible parody of him. Pieced together from memories and pictures. Stitched in place through wretched red lines that wept in shivers.

Asking her to come join him.

Down the hole.

She couldn't help it. As paralysed as she was before, now she was a puppet for something else. The hole.

As she stepped over the edge, gravity took over.

Greg smiled. Too wide.

And Hannah screamed. In her bed, drenched in sweat.

She wasn't alone. In his room next door, Warren was wailing, with Jarelle assisting in a muted chorus. Across Anton Court, lights flicked on as various residents found themselves waking from an assortment of twisted vignettes.

Outside, the hole simply sat there.

Open.

Quiet.

DAY 4

The weekend had arrived, lacking all the delight that it usually brought.

The peace and fun that Hannah would have with her boys was gone by the time the sun peaked in the sky. Louise had come to her door and announced that she and Tim were taking HP Properties' offer to stay at the Garry Hotel. Her reasons were sound enough; she was scared for Samantha's safety around the hole.

She questioned whether Hannah and the boys would join them.

It was an obvious decision. The safety of Jarelle and Warren were naturally paramount to Hannah, and after yesterday's concerns over the lack of protection the residents had from the hole, the sanctuary of the hotel was the only right decision.

And yet, Hannah couldn't bring herself to leave.

Part of that was the pride in her home, and her reluctance to hand it so easily to HP Properties. It was a paranoia that defied logic, in many ways, but one that she couldn't remove from her mind. The other thing was that the hole intrigued her. She wanted to see how things ended.

A thought that confused even her in what it meant.

Luckily, once their bags were packed, the boys saw it as a holiday. They seemed to get a certain glee from being away from their mother for a period, seeing it as a free pass to behave however they wanted. Sure, they'd be under the watchful eye of the Coopers, and Hannah would come see them, but it was still seen in their eyes as an exciting adventure away from home.

To her disgust, Hannah saw it as a respite.

Her convincing herself that this was for the best was reinforced when they all left. Even as their small steps went toward Tim's car, both Jarelle and

Warren seemed to linger too long toward the hole, their saunter moving too close to the edge. It was like a lure had been thrown out and slowly dragged back toward the abyss, and the boys were helpless to resist it.

Luckily, Hannah's firm tone distracted them long enough to snap out of it and get in the car.

There was one more addition to the exodus; Charles, Hannah's comrade-in-goss, was on his way as well. To anyone listening, he bragged about the chance to indulge in the Hotel's spa and live the life of the decadent that he always felt he was. In truth, as he confided to Hannah, it was far more bitter.

"I can't be too close to that... horridness," he said to her away from the crowd.

"Why not?"

"My darling, only two people know what I'm about to tell you, William and my therapist. Lovely lady, very caring. Anyhoo, I have a history of being rather... fickle. With my life. And a rather big hole like that? It's too much of a temptation, if you understand?"

Hannah did understand. When Charles told her about the dreams he'd been having, she understood even more.

The hole wasn't just an ugly new feature of the Court, it was infecting them all.

It just seemed like some were stronger than others to resist its allure.

And so, away they went, to enjoy some quality pampering time at the Garry Hotel. There, they would indulge in everything under HP Properties' ticket, without any further cares in the world.

Meanwhile, the rest of them would have a rather large care.

One that was now six and half feet wide.

This was a riddle that even Crendon couldn't solve. For him, the hole was that spot that no matter how much you squeezed, it never popped. It just remained there, a blemish forever taunting him. Unlike the residents, he could not just grab a few belongings and wander off to relax; he was the site manager, the face of HP Properties and the one who would continue to face the wrath of The Colonel, himself conspicuous by his absence. Hannah felt a bit sorry for him, watching as he saw off the Coopers.

She'd never done it before, but she felt like reaching out to him.

"You OK?"

The question seemed to throw him. His eye lingered on her a few too many times, but now she was coming to him, it threw him for a loop.

"Fine."

"I've noticed. I'm friends with Jack too," Hannah said, referring to their tipple of choice.

Then a rare thing happened. Crendon cracked a smile. Not a cynical one, nor a sneer, a genuine amused smile.

It didn't last long.

"You know I've tried, right? The Colonel thinks I'm being lazy but... I have tried."

Hannah knew, but Crendon needed to vent.

"I've tried filling it, I've tried covering it, and now... well now, they're taking charge. And you know what they want to do?"

"What?"

Crendon turned with an incredulous look. "They want to bloody go down it."

Hannah couldn't believe this.

"They want *you* to go *down* it?"

"Not me, thank fuck. But someone has asked them and they've positively snapped at the idea."

Hannah knew who would request such a thing. She turned round and saw Rich with his arms around Stacey, pulling her close to the wretched pit. He looked excited, even a little manic.

She wasn't feeling the same.

Crendon shook his head.

"I don't want this, Hannah."

"I know," she said, distracted by Rich's reckless tomfoolery.

"It's not what I signed up for. It's just..."

Before he could say anymore, Crendon's phone rang and Hannah saw that it was from his masters.

HP Properties.

As the site manager was called to his infernal duties, Hannah looked back to where Rich and Stacey were now returning home, and noticed Rich's longing look at the hole. The man was excited.

Hannah felt sick.

Of all the people in Anton Court, the only person who hadn't been asked about their reaction to what was happening was a certain Mrs Heather Stanley.

Hannah decided, with William's help, to change that.

The two of them conferred and decided to go round together, looking to make peace with the beleaguered wife of The Colonel. While he ranted and raved, Heather stayed in the background, a shrinking violet in a world full of deep purples.

It was just the way her generation were, it seemed.

So Hannah threw together some form of gift-basket – consisting of a few boxes of tea and biscuits - while William armed himself with something a little bit finer on the palate. Hannah looked at the cheeses, and wondered aloud whether a woman of Heather's lifestyle had need for chocolate straight from Belgium.

"Hannah, everyone needs chocolate," William said.

She couldn't argue with that.

Talking of argument, the one obstacle that prevented them from bonding with Heather – The Colonel – was not in the vicinity. Despite the letter from HP Properties, he had still left first thing in the morning to hold crisis talks with someone, presumed to be the local council. It was to be a futile gesture, given everything so far, but The Colonel was nothing if not determined. A man with his experiences isn't expected to be anything but.

When Heather answered the door, she seemed a bit taken aback.

After a strong cup of tea amongst her highly maintained back garden, she seemed to relax a bit more.

"He just cares," she said.

"That's certainly one word," William said.

"We've always kept quiet, as you know, but also made sure not to seem too… aloof. We did send you a card, after all, Hannah."

They had. Everyone in the Court had after Greg had gone. Even though they barely knew each other.

It was just the done thing.

That aside, the Stanleys were definitely in the 'keep to themselves' mould. Heather kept pointing out that they didn't intend to be rude, and actually shone a light on her tense husband. The conflicts he had served in – Falklands, Northern Ireland, the Gulf – had left him with enough PTSD to wind anyone up to breaking point, but his insistence on a stiff upper lip and refusal to show weakness meant that his personality had turned more aggressive than anything else. Which, of course, prompted all the wrong questions.

"He doesn't... you know," Hannah said, not wanting to say the words Domestic Abuse.

"Oh Lord, no. I mean, I can see why... but oh no. Never! James is quite the gentleman really."

Her smile suggested more things about The Colonel than anyone had ever dared ask. In fact, looking at the pictures that Heather willingly showed Hannah and William, you saw a man who was not just proud, but incredibly loving. Every picture of him and Heather had a wide smile across his face, and when he was looking at her, eyes shining so brightly it almost eclipsed the whole image.

It was a stark difference to the raging warrior they had always seen.

"This business has triggered him, I fear," Heather said. "He was always highly strung, as you know, but this... this seems to have changed him somewhat."

Another victim of the hole's subconscious hate plague, Hannah thought.

The hole to The Colonel wasn't just a crater in the ground, it was an invasion, Heather told them. It was an abomination that threatened his way of life, and The Colonel was taking out his rage on Crendon and HP Properties.

"He doesn't mean to be so angry at poor Vincent, but he doesn't know what else to do. He seems... confused."

"Is he alright?" William said. It was a question that hadn't actually been thought of yet.

Before Heather could answer, the man himself clicked his key in the lock, and opened the door to see the visitors surveying his home. For a moment, Hannah thought that a fresh riot was about to break out, but instead was surprised to see The Colonel look at them with fire in his eyes, and then that fire immediately be doused when he looked at Heather.

"Any news?" he said, his voice lacking the vitriol of normal.

Heather shook her head, and The Colonel hung his coat on the rack, and went upstairs.

"I best see if he's alright," she said to Hannah and William, before seeing them off for the afternoon. The two wandered down the Stanleys front path, and looked over to the hole.

There, Rich was in conference with Crendon.

With one looking far happier than the other.

"You have no liability, Vinnie."

Crendon wasn't easily convinced by Rich's smooth talking. He'd seen men like him before; he knew that they were blessed with the gift of the gab but lacking in anything resembling common sense. This was painfully evident in the fact that Rich wanted to go down the hole.

And HP had gleefully OK'd it.

"Aren't you curious? About what's down there?"

"It's a hole, Mr Davis."

"But *why* is it a hole? Where's it *come* from? What's *down* there?"

Crendon saw Hannah and William approaching and used this as his cue to go.

Albeit with one last comment.

"Nobody cares, Rich. Nobody but you."

This comment didn't sting as much as Crendon hoped it would. Mostly because both men knew this wasn't true. The residents *did* want to know what was down there.

Including Crendon.

"You're really going down there?" Hannah said.

Rich noticed his new audience, and puffed up his chest in the best way a braggart could. "Damn right. An adventurer can't turn down an opportunity that lands on his own doorstep."

"I thought you were a tech wizard," William said.

"Even Indiana Jones was a humble archaeologist."

Hannah looked down the hole and felt sick at the sheer depth of the thing. Every time she looked down, she felt this horrible pull, a force that wanted her to go down there. A force that beckoned her to see for herself what was at the bottom. It didn't excite her like it did Rich Davis.

It terrified her.

"I reckon it's a few thousand feet deep, maybe more," Rich said. "And if it is? Boy, that's exciting, don't you think?"

"It's a hole," Hannah said, backing away before the pull won its mental tug-of-war.

"Never been spelunking, Han?"

She shook her head and tried to smile politely.

"There's something absolutely thrilling about diving into the great unknown. The maw of nature, open and ready for you to see what lurks beneath. What monsters there are waiting for you, never before seen?"

The last part drew a sick smile from Rich, which William immediately picked up on.

"You know monsters don't exist, Richard?"

"How do you know?"

"I grew up."

Rich laughed, not realising the acid in the sentiment.

"I've got a mate on the way, real rugged type. Maybe not *your* type, Will."

It was William's turn to smile politely.

"If any of you want to join in, just let me know. Could be a real story to tell."

"What about Stacey?" Hannah said.

Rich's smile withered a bit, as he just dismissed this with a wave.

"Stacey isn't the adventurous type."

It was the sort of comment that suggested he meant more than just potholing. In the time they'd lived on Anton Court, Rich and Stacey's relationship had been... less than stable. And judging by the visitors they had when the other wasn't there, they both knew it.

Even Hannah had to turn down multiple offers to 'hang' with Rich. One being only two days after Greg had died.

"Enjoy your hole, Rich," she said, wandering back to her home.

"Sure I can't tempt you to dive in? Break the monotony?"

She was sure. For now, she was happy to watch.

Mostly out of fear for how far that pit went down.

And if monsters did exist.

Rich's friend Quinn arrived a few hours later.

He was your typical Alpha Bro; hair bleached badly enough to show the roots, sunglasses preventing any sort of eye contact, and a goatee beard trimmed to the point of obsession. Despite the climate, he hopped out of his truck dressed in a shirt that was too bright, and shorts that were too short.

And Hannah thought Rich was bad.

The two embraced in the kind of elaborate embrace that men of their type think is 'cool'. After this routine, the business of the hole came up.

Right away, Quinn was impressed.

"How did you get this beauty?"

"Just popped up a few days ago," Rich said, standing proud like he had made the hole himself.

"And you left it this long to tell me?"

"Call it a surprise."

The two men scouted the circumference of the hole, with Quinn bending down and feeling the ridge. He commented on what the residents of Anton Court already knew – that the wall of the hole was far too smooth to be naturally occurring. In fact, his palm was stained black, like it was ash.

Unlike poor Ronnie, though, his hand remained in one piece.

"Tried any lights?"

"Been waiting for your gear."

Quinn nodded and went back to his truck. He threw a big sack to the ground, and reached inside to produce a long cylinder that Hannah recognised as a flare. With a quick snap of the stick, a bright light was produced and soon faded as it fell into the abyss.

Hannah couldn't see exactly what the men saw, but judging by how impressed they appeared, it was quite something.

"Fuck me, Rich, you might have something here."

"You think?" Rich said, still smug.

"I think? This thing makes the Trench look like a bloody pothole."

Another high five was shared, as the two men celebrated their discovery.

From there, it was a case of watching the two set themselves up for a descent. Hannah watched intently as ropes were produced, harnesses were tested, and more flares were readied to crack when necessary. What really caught her eye was the massive reel on the back of Quinn's truck. For now, it just sat idly, but the sheer amount of rope spun around it was enough to give her the impression that this wasn't just a hobby for the bleached bro.

This was serious business.

When Quinn saw Hannah watching, his eyes sparkled and suddenly she was being convinced to be part of the crew. Not wanting to be left alone with these two, she demurred at first before calling in William to assist. Thankfully, Crendon soon emerged from his home, looking to assert himself over proceedings.

Rich, ever the big kid, was eager to show the site manager what they'd discovered.

"Look at this," he said, before snapping a flare and throwing it down the hole.

The five of them watched as the flare fell deeper into the hole, going from a bright burn before turning into something resembling a dull ember.

At first, nobody was really that impressed, and then Quinn quoted the numbers.

"You know how far that is?"

"Go on," Crendon said.

"Twelve. Thousand. Fucking. Feet."

There were no words. Not even an audible exclamation. Hannah, William and Crendon just looked down the hole, while Rich and Quinn got very excited.

12,000 feet. Straight down.

William summed it up best.

"This hasn't been done by gas."

"In that case," Hannah said, "what the Hell has done it?"

In celebration, Rich threw another flare down the hole. After a few minutes, it was once again gone.

He giggled.

"Twelve thousand feet…"

Listening to the two explorers talk, the world record for distance in caving was over 7000 feet. The Veryovkina Cave, based in the former soviet country of Georgia, was explored by a couple of Russians looking to collect samples of never before seen fauna.

With this particular descent, the idea wasn't for the benefit of science, it was for the benefit of one very rich adventurer. The idea that the hole would blow the Russian expedition out the water only added to Rich and Quinn's excitement.

The two men adopted very different mentalities, though. While Rich was eager to jump in the hole and start abseiling down, Quinn knew better. This was why Rich had brought him in, knowing his experience and professionalism – that in all honesty was malleable when it came to money – would help things go smoothly. It wasn't just a case of wrapping a rope around the waist and diving in, proper procedures had to be undertaken.

As Hannah, William, and a vaguely bitter Crendon watched, Quinn spoke about various things such as tensile strength and descent speed that sailed over most of their heads. Rich listened intently, but it was apparent from his nods that he was equally blasé about what it all meant.

What did grab the attention was what Quinn had brought with him. On the back of a large, flatbed truck, was essentially a large cable reel. Made of steel rather than wood, and housing thick, red rope, it was anchored to the truck via several heavy-duty bolts and counterweights. It seemed a bit overkill to Hannah, but William was on hand to explain that even with Rich's slight weight, the deeper he'd go the more pressure he'd put on the reel.

All this was starting to wear on Rich. His manic excitement had been tempered down into barely restrained shuffling, his whole body bopping along to a beat only he could hear. He turned to Hannah and smiled.

"Sure I can't tempt you to jump in?"

"You want me to go down a twelve thousand feet hole with you?"

"You had a better first date offer?"

"Don't you have a girlfriend?"

Rich looked round and saw Stacey appear from their home. He smiled at Hannah, but she could see his heart wasn't in it.

Whatever blood was flowing, it was now safely out of any annoying areas.

As Stacey became intrigued by what was happening, Rich outlined in very basic terms what he was about to embark on with Quinn. Naturally, she wanted to join in, but unlike Hannah, wasn't deemed worthy enough.

Instead, she was given a credit card, and asked to keep herself busy. Being the strong, independent woman she was, she obliged and left them all to it.

"Lovely girl," Crendon said.

"She's all yours."

Rich offered Hannah a wink.

She offered to push him in.

While almost tempted, Rich carried on with his explanation of his journey. Quinn would truss him up and allow a slow, steady descent down the hole. While moving down, Rich would be armed with a torch and the odd supply, making sure to use the sides of the hole to maintain balance. To the layman it all sounded rather important and serious, but to a man like William it was mere bluster.

Finally, it was time.

The original plan was for Quinn to go down first with Rich following, but a hefty financial bonus changed that. Instead, Rich now sat alone on the edge of the hole, trussed up and connected to the giant reel behind him. Quinn made sure everything was secure and set up, before giving the thumbs up.

And with a wink to Hannah, Rich slipped in.

"Have you got a knife?" she asked Quinn.

"Why?"

"No reason."

Armed with his torch, Rich shined it as best he could down the hole. Much like the flare before it, the ebony walls of the pit ate up the light into oblivion, meaning there was only a few feet of illumination at best. Still, this didn't deter Rich, and he carefully walked his way down with his feet pushing against the wall, and his back against the opposite side.

The curious thing that William noted was despite Rich's body applying itself hard against the walls, no debris seemed to crumble off. He confirmed that it was as smooth as it looked as well, almost sliding down at times instead of walking.

Also, it seemed to taper as it got deeper. Despite only being a few feet down, Rich had noticed the full extent of his body begin to crouch inward.

30 minutes later, and Rich was barely visible. A vague ember the only clue to his presence in the hole.

"You really believe it's that deep?" William asked Quinn.

The Aussie smiled.

"But… twelve thousand feet? That's over two miles."

"Tell me about it, mate. Gift of a lifetime."

The three Court locals stood with a slight feeling of unease, which was counter to Quinn's own excitement. Occasionally, Crendon would peek down the hole, then back away with a shiver, only to confirm he could still see the light. Then, Quinn asked the question on everybody's mind.

"So how did it get here?"

Nobody could answer. In their minds, they didn't want to answer; such was the chill of the unknowable.

Another 15 minutes passed, and the decision was made to haul Rich back up.

Once his head popped over the hole's edge, he smiled.

"We're gonna need radios," he said, looking like he was having the time of his life.

At least someone was.

As dusk drew in, the mood in Anton Court was feverish. Rich was as excited as ever about the prospect of his hole-based adventure, something that was shared vicariously by Quinn. Stacey was also gleeful about Rich's plans, mostly because that meant he would be out of her hair.

While the fever within the Davis residence was joyful, the other houses were infected with something more akin to a chill. The enjoyment Rich got out of the idea of exploring the hole evoked concern and paranoia in others. Crendon was the most obvious, his ear constantly attached to his phone while HP Properties informed him of the latest updates. Everyone expected

The Colonel to be more vocal, but since his visit to the council his attitude had become less boisterous and more brooding. While this would usually be agreeable in others, with The Colonel it was more foreboding.

Even Heather looked more worried than usual.

Then there was Hannah. She had a bit of small talk with William before he went to make sure Charles was settling in, but once left alone she felt the tension that the hole seemed to press upon her. It wasn't just the bad dreams it seemed to instigate within her, it was the fact that now it had taken away her children.

Of course, she knew that there was nothing stopping her from being at the hotel with them. Nothing aside from her own paranoia at losing her home, and her growing need to see what was down the damn hole.

It didn't help hearing their voices over the phone. Hannah listened as they talked about the ice cream they'd eaten, the giant swimming pool the hotel had with all the water slides and fountains, and the fun they were having with the Coopers.

Then Warren asked when she was coming.

Hannah wanted to pack a bag and get the first taxi out of there. She wanted to leave Rich and Quinn to slather over their hole. She wanted the Court to be behind her.

But then her own stubborn nature sank its talons into her, and she stayed in her home. Alone.

She hated herself for it.

Despite the assurances that Greg's employers gave her, despite the evidence they provided to show they were covering the costs of her residency within Anton Court, and despite the fact they almost mocked the idea of HP Properties challenging them, it all seemed moot in reality. Hannah was painfully aware of the passive aggressive threats HP had made toward her - the comments toward her status as a single mother, how a more inclusive neighbourhood would surely be better for her children.

Plenty of bullshit doublespeak said behind a painted smile.

It was then that she considered the reaction of HP Properties toward the hole. It seemed to her like they were actually protective of it, for some reason. Crendon's actions in trying to fill or cover it had earned their ire, and their iron grip over the Court's privacy meant that no police or council authority would be brought in to investigate themselves.

Legally, it seemed suspect as hell. But somehow, they were doing it.

And now, the cherry on top of their damned sundae was the fact they had a willing volunteer in Rich to go down the damn thing.

But then Hannah laughed. All of these thoughts were just the paranoia dancing in her brain. Conspiracy theories conjured by an overactive mind that was bored by loneliness and an oxymoronic feeling of forced strength and overwhelming weakness.

Hannah didn't cry, and she was determined not to start now.

Despite the tears rolling down her cheeks.

She told Jarelle and Warren she loved them, and promised to see them soon. To her, this didn't seem like an empty promise; it felt like something she had to say. There was a feeling, an atmosphere in the air, that she had to make pledges like that. That nagging feeling in the back of her mind was growing louder each day, demanding to be heard.

At that moment, the lion inside Hannah's mind roared.

Screw paranoia. Screw HP Properties. And most importantly, screw the damn hole outside. She wasn't going to let such things keep her away from her kids. She wasn't going to be pushed around by stupid thoughts and petty bureaucrats. And she certainly wasn't going to let a damn hole run her life.

With a furious determination that had been lacking for too long, Hannah packed her bags and called a taxi.

She was going to see her children.

DAY 5

The whole thing had gone exactly how Hannah had wanted it to.

While it wasn't obscenely late, she had arrived at the Garry Hotel far beyond the boys' usual bedtime. Some conspiring had taken place between Hannah and the Coopers, and so on top of their joy at being able to stay up and continue playing, Jarelle and Warren were even more overjoyed at their mother knocking at their door.

Exhaustion soon overwhelmed them all, and the last thing Hannah remembered was both her sons cuddling up to her on a plush, king-size bed, and her own consciousness slipping away peacefully for what felt like the first time in months. When the sun finally rose, it struck her full in the face thanks to an open curtain, and the warmth made Hannah smile.

The Hotel itself was a grand affair; situated behind gates that made the ones to Anton Court seem common. A long, lavish driveway took you past rows of exotic flowers, beyond which lay a variety of tennis courts, outdoor swimming pools, and gardens. Standing proudly in the middle of all this was the Garry Hotel itself, several stories high and looking more like a private manor than a place to lay your head.

As breakfast was had in the expansive dining room, another guest looked pleased by Hannah's presence. Charles immediately came over and gave her a big hug, and extolled the many ways to get pampered in the hotel. Everything he said helped boost Hannah's mood and convince her she had made the right decision. That staying at Anton Court would only exacerbate her fragile mental health.

She would have remained in this positive state as well, until William turned up.

It wasn't his fault, but as one of the Court residents who had firmly stayed behind, he was also a courier of news for recent developments. And recent developments were not good.

"He's going right down there," William said over a strong coffee.

"And how far is that?" Charles said, looking far more serious than Hannah would have thought.

"Not a clue. They've already estimated five miles, but…"

Even though Hannah sat with the Barretts, she wasn't seen as an active participant in their conversation. In fact, she felt more like an intruder, especially at times when William would pause, remember she was there, and smile politely.

When Warren came over and started tugging at her top to show her something, it was seen by all as the perfect opportunity for her to break away.

Whether she wanted to or not.

Still, it was her job as a mother to attend to her boys. They were, after all, the reason she had come to the hotel. They were also much more than that, being the last connective thread to Greg. She saw his eyes in both of them, although Jarelle resembled him far more than Warren did. At times it unnerved her as she caught a fleeting glimpse of Jarelle in the shadows and had to remind herself that her love was, indeed, still dead. To their credit, the boys had handled their father's death well.

But that was probably due to the fact they did not understand it yet.

Still, whilst sitting and watching he two boys demolish a plate full of random items from the breakfast buffet, Hannah listened intently as they talked about all the cool stuff they'd seen and done, and how 'awesome' their room was.

"I can't believe we got our own room," Jarelle said. While this was true, it was annexed from Tim and Louise's room, so they weren't quite as independent as they thought.

"It's huge," Warren said. "Much bigger than our one at home."

As he said that, Warren went from a state of hyperactivity, to a sudden pout.

"I miss my room."

"It's my room too."

"Yeah, well I miss it more than you."

"I miss my room too," Hannah said, the words hurting as they came out, but the smile on her face refusing to be broken by such solemn thoughts. The more the boys raved about their stay, the more proud Hannah felt. They were growing up so fast, and a 'holiday' such as this only proved their on-going maturity. Jarelle would be a teenager soon, and Hannah remembered how spirited she was at that age.

She always joked to Greg that she hoped they inherited his calm.

She missed that.

Their serenity was suddenly broken by the clatter of fist upon table. Along with the Coopers, Hannah turned to see an embarrassed Charles looking back.

"Sorry, darlings," he said. "You know me."

Naturally, this outburst spawned the seeds of gossip, and Hannah now found herself in conversation with Louise.

"What do you think they're talking about?"

Hannah knew, but was reluctant to say.

"Probably nothing."

"It doesn't look like nothing…"

This was true. Even from across the room, the firm glances between the Barretts were heated enough to sense all was not right. William had always been the more level-headed one in the relationship, and witnessing his stoicism in the face of Charles's flamboyance was an exercise in how to deal with hysteria.

It wouldn't be long until the bough broke.

And Tim ended up being the one to break it.

"Everything OK, chaps?" he said, walking over to their table.

"Everything's fine," William said, smiling easily.

"Splendid," Charles spat.

"Will, why don't you come to the hotel as well? Then we can all get together and…"

"He won't stay."

Charles glared at William, who didn't blink.

"Are you sure? Because…"

Before Tim could stammer on, Hannah appeared.

"He wants to see Rich go down the hole."

Now the truth was out, there was no longer any need to play dumb and hide their hands. William took a deep breath, nodded, and rose from the table.

"Call it professional curiosity," he said, "but I feel my being there can only be a positive thing."

"And I say we need to call in the professionals," Charles said.

To everyone's surprise, it was William's turn to stare daggers at his husband. Hannah had never seen such a look from him before, and did not care to ever see it again.

"HP are already planning to come to the Court, and when they do…"

"HP are coming?" Hannah said.

Suddenly, every paranoid thought and negative scenario flooded her mind as if a mental dam had broken. With HP Properties coming to Anton Court, that meant her home was unguarded and they could do any number of things to it. Change the locks, board the windows, take it away from her.

"I need to go back," Hannah said, staring into space.

"What?" Charles said.

"I can't... I just..."

"Oh, Hannah..."

Hannah looked at her boys, happily playing with their food at the table, and looked back at William. He looked as serious as she feared, especially with the news that HP Properties were en route.

"It's got you, hasn't it my dear?"

Hannah didn't say anything. She couldn't.

She didn't need to.

"It has a hold on you, doesn't it? Like a lure..."

Tim coughed to interrupt.

"Um, I must admit it did seem quite... interesting..."

"And the dreams, tell them about the dreams," Louise said.

"Let me guess," William said. "Loved one calling you in? Jumping into the hole? Falling?"

"Forever," Charles said.

The adults stood quietly, listening to the sound of their children, blissfully unaware of their shared horror. Without saying a word, Hannah agreed to go with William back to Anton Court, and part of her knew that she wouldn't experience the steam room or the aromatic massages that Charles spoke of.

In truth, even he knew this would happen eventually.

"It has claws," he said, smiling weakly. "Once they dig in, they're very hard to pry out."

It sounded absurd, but made perfect sense to everyone. The Coopers remained strong, focussing more on looking after Samantha and Hannah's boys, rather than giving in to the mystery of the hole.

Charles could see, in both his husband and his best friend, that the hole had already whittled away at their own strength.

He stood up, embraced William with a long hug and loving kiss, before turning to Hannah.

"Oh, I wish Greg was still here," he said.

"Me too," Hannah said.

As they broke away, she again noticed the firm look William directed at Charles. He didn't really care, and instead kept his eyes on Hannah.

"Promise me you won't do anything stupid."

"Like go down the hole?"

Hannah laughed, but Charles remained serious.

"I'll leave that to Rich," she said.

Charles closed his eyes, smiled, and hugged Hannah hard again. By the time awkward goodbyes were said and more false promises were given to her boys, William had started his car and left a door open for Hannah to enter.

As they drove away, she looked back and felt rotten.

Not because she was leaving her children behind.

But because she was more excited about going back to the hole.

Upon arriving back to Anton Court, Hannah was greeted by quite the sight.

In the short time she had been away from her home the Court had turned from a quiet residential area to a small-scale operation. Quinn's truck blocked the majority of the community's main gate, with its gigantic reel still sitting high on the vehicle's bed. Quinn himself was by the side, a laptop positioned on a small table that he attended to with deep concentration. While he did this, Rich was hobnobbing with a man in a suit.

A man that made Hannah feel sick.

There was no doubt he was an employee of HP Properties. He had that pale, slimy look to him - all over-gelled hair and angular cheekbones. As William steered aside the truck, Hannah had a brief exchange of looks with the man, whose smile seeped across his face.

Of course, Crendon was there as well, but he was rendered impotent by the fact his superiors were here. All he could do was stand there and listen as Rich detailed his plans with the HP Properties suit. Once William was parked up, Hannah got out the car quickly and made sure to make her way to the conference. As she did so, she made sure to take in the rest of the Court; sure enough, The Colonel was watching intently from the safety of his home, Heather behind him, and Stacey was looking bored from Rich's abode.

Hannah's blood chilled as she saw someone looking over her property.

"Can I help you?" she said, not bothering to hide the venom in her tone.

The woman, dressed in less formal wear than the suit but still looking more important than Crendon, took note of Hannah's swift approach and attempted to stutter out an explanation. Before any words could leave her lips, a voice spoke up.

"That'll be all for now, Irene."

Irene did her best to smile, but was obviously intimidated by Hannah. Watching the strange woman scurry away, she saw that the HP Properties representative was making his way over.

"Are you Danforth?" Hannah said.

"I'm afraid not. The name is Norris, I work alongside Danforth in monitoring our properties here on Anton Court."

"And why was she 'monitoring' my home?"

"Well, Miss Suggs, we believed you had abandoned it."

There was no attempt on the part of Norris to disguise his false allegation, and Hannah knew it. For some reason, her paranoia was coming true and all her fears were encapsulated in this seedy figure before her.

"I was taking up *your* invite," she said, staring murder at Norris.

"I see. Again, though, your situation combined with the current one developing," Norris said, motioning to the hole, "means that perhaps a change is the best option?"

"I'm not leaving my house."

"I understand. But consider this…"

"I pay my bills."

Norris scoffed. "Now, Miss Suggs, we both know *you* don't pay your bills."

Hannah was shaking by this point. How dare this piece of shit simply stride into Anton Court and declare her no longer suitable? How dare HP Properties think that, because her partner died, she wasn't capable of maintaining her presence there?

She couldn't help but feel there were more reasons beyond the perceived "shame" of her being an unemployed single mother.

And a widow at that.

As her knuckles tightened and teeth bared ever more form behind her lips, Norris was saved by the inquiring mind of Rich Davis. As he jogged over, forever smiling those bright, white teeth he had paid handsomely for, he made sure to nod neighbourly at Hannah.

"Glad to see you're back, Han," he said.

Hannah didn't say anything. She was doing everything she could to maintain her composure.

"Everything alright?"

"We were just discussing Miss Suggs's residency here on Anton Court," Norris said. "Especially given current events."

"Ah, don't worry about the hole," Rich said. "I'm getting to the bottom of it. Literally!"

Amused by his own pun, Rich laughed heartily while guiding Norris away from the furious Hannah. As the two went back to their conference close to the hole, she turned toward her front door and angrily threw it open, slamming the door behind her.

She made no attempt to hide the primal scream she let out once she was inside.

"Don't worry. We're aware."

Perry sounded calm, but it wasn't transferring to Hannah. After the encounter with Norris, she had called Greg's former employer and in a fit of paranoia-fuelled mania, demanded to speak to her confidante. After much screaming and cursing, she had been put through.

"It's not enough you're aware, Perry! They want to take my fucking home!"

"They won't take your home."

"But they're here! Now! Fucking…"

"Hannah, calm down," Perry said. "The position they're taking is that the property was under Greg's name, and that you were simply a… an additional tenant. Family that didn't need to be named under contract. When he died, their argument is that the contract ended."

"But…"

"But it didn't, I know. It was transferred to you, his widow. Except, they are contesting this. The problem is, they have to contest this with the guarantor of Greg's housing contract."

"Who is…?"

"Us."

Hannah could feel Perry smiling down the phone. Even though she still didn't know who "us" were, she was confident that they actually gave a shit about her. Especially when they were so calm in the face of her growing stress.

"I'm sorry," Hannah said, finally letting the tension in her body begin to melt. "It's just… this hole… Greg…"

"It's a tough time, we understand that," Perry said. "And remember, we are always here for you. I'm always on the other end of the phone, and if required, can be there within minutes."

"Thank you. I…"

"Your boys are at the hotel, correct?"

The mention of her children made Hannah begin to shake again.

"Yes."

"Do you want to go stay with them, or…"

As much as she hated the answer, Hannah knew the power of how she felt in that moment was too much to fight against.

"Again, I understand," Perry said. "Tell you what I'll do. I'll send one of my colleagues to go make sure they are cared for…"

"The Coopers are…"

"The Coopers are lovely people, and doing a fine job, but I feel we need to treat Jarelle and Warren, don't we?"

Hannah managed to break into a smile.

"And if you can't be there physically, we can work on ways to make sure you're there… digitally."

Again, none of what Perry was saying made any real sense, but by now Hannah was too blitzed to really argue or ask questions. Instead, she just continued whispering her thanks, until Perry could take control of the call.

"Greg was a fine man, Hannah. It was a tragedy what happened. But just because he's passed, doesn't mean he's gone. Not in your eyes, not in your children's, and definitely not in ours. As far as we're concerned, Greg is still a member of our team."

"I don't know what to say…"

"You don't need to say anything. Just… continue being aware."

Hannah was confused. The unease that had begun to drift away was surging back into her synapses.

"Aware of what?"

"The hole," Perry said, and ended things there.

Outside, the excitement was coming to a boil.

Rich had been trussed up securely by Quinn as Norris watched alongside Crendon. William also was keeping a keen eye on the events as they unfolded, while The Colonel made up the rest of the audience from the safety of his home. As Hannah came out to join them, she noted how the whole scene was being treated as some sort of lark, a Boys Own adventure that couldn't possibly go wrong.

The gear affixed to Rich looked serious enough, though. Despite the frivolity Rich showed in his eagerness to drop down the hole, Quinn was still a professional, and applied a stern approach to making sure his client/friend wouldn't suffer any unforeseen accidents. The truss wrapped around Rich was fixed with several safety clips and back-ups, while a chest mounted camera looked up at him from a small rucksack filled with supplies.

On the drive back to Anton Court, William had shared the true horror of what was unfolding. Rich was determined to reach the bottom of the hole, and vowed not to come out until he had done so. Given the sheer depth of the thing, there were questions as to whether there even *was* a bottom to it, an absurd suggestion that seemed strangely possible. While Quinn checked on the strength of the cable that would slowly lower Rich down, Hannah looked over at Norris as he spoke firmly to Crendon. The caretaker didn't seem to like what he was hearing, but did not argue back.

Everything seemed quite surreal at that moment.

For a moment, Hannah felt like returning back to the hotel. Back to where her boys were.

But as Rich strode confidently to the edge of the hole, she knew she couldn't leave. Not until she saw how this ended.

"All great adventures start with a single step," Rich said, his back to the hole. "But not this time."

Suddenly, he jumped backward and vanished down the hole. Only the slipping hiss of the rope unfurling indicating his descent.

There was less shock than expected, although from her balcony Stacey had let out a slight scream. Everyone else just let their heart skip a beat, before the eerie calm of the day fell back into place. Even Norris, the on-site evaluator from HP Properties, simply said a few final words to Crendon before going to leave.

Before he could, a familiar dissenting voice spoke up.

"You're just letting this happen?"

As Norris turned his attention to The Colonel, now marching forth toward the HP representative, Crendon joined the others in tense anticipation of what was about to unfold.

"If you have a problem..."

"If I have a problem? You just let a man jump down a damn hole!"

"Under full supervision from experts..." Norris said, indicating toward an uncomfortable Quinn.

"Expert or not, this is irresponsible."

The way The Colonel's voice changed from a loud bluster to a muted growl caused shivers to ripple through Hannah. This wasn't just rage coming from the old man, this was something far more terrifying.

"I recommend you contact our complaints department, Mr Stanley..."

"There is no complaints department, *Mr* Norris."

To the surprise of those watching, Norris couldn't answer. A few stammers and aborted thoughts echoed through his expression, but no real words came from his lips.

"Nothing?" The Colonel said.

Conceding his point, Norris simply huffed and adjusted his suit.

"Exactly, Mr Stanley," he said. "There's nothing *you* can do."

As Norris made a quick escape to his waiting car, the tension of the scene was suddenly broken by a very chipper voice.

"Hello from below!"

Everyone turned to where Quinn stood, a screen set up next to him on the back of the truck. Behind it, the cable was slowly unravelling, giving more and more length into the hole.

On the screen, lit up by a faint flashlight, was Rich's face.

He looked so happy.

And apart from Quinn, he was the only one.

Looking down the hole, you could see the faint light of Rich's torch illuminate the walls of the pit. The further he went down, the more the darkness swallowed that light up. The smooth, tar-like walls gave nothing back in terms of reflection, meaning that the further Rich went, the less they saw of him.

His camera was now the only real contact they had with him; a tiny camera strapped around his chest, producing either a very unflattering selfie or whatever Rich himself was looking at. At that point, he had positioned the lens to showcase his surroundings, shiny, onyx surfaces that were smooth to the touch and very difficult to illuminate.

Luckily, Rich didn't suffer the same fate that Crendon's friend Ronnie had when touching the hole's walls; no flesh was burnt from his digits, with Rich in fact saying that it didn't feel like soil or earth. Instead, it felt man made, a perfectly sleek surface that didn't yield no matter how hard he poked at it.

It wasn't the scientific method William would use, but it was interesting enough.

The science behind the hole didn't hold Hannah's attention, though. Instead, she listened in as Quinn conferred with Rich. The wannabe adventurer spoke in more detail about what the inside of the hole felt like, telling those listening that it seemed to have a constant, ambient temperature, one that was cool, but not cold. Dressed in only a simple T-shirt and jeans, Rich didn't show any discomfort with his surroundings, with the only shaking coming from the instability of the camera as he abseiled further down.

At one stage, Rich leaned back, and showed his point of view toward the surface. By now, the only thing he could see was a small aperture barely allowing any light in to help guide him. The only assistance to his eyes was the small flashlight attached to the camera, which most of the time saw only black anyway.

"How deep you thinking so far?" Quinn said.

"Not hit flare point yet," Rich said, making reference to their earlier research. "So far, I can't see anything resembling a surface, though. In fact there's no alcoves or divergence from the walls going straight down."

Quinn looked up to the sky, wrinkled his face, and then looked into the camera.

"Getting late," he said to the laptop in front of him, something that felt more natural than looking down the hole. "You sure you want to keep the cable moving at this speed?"

Rich was certain. For the sake of safety his descent was being maintained at a steady speed to prevent any unforeseen structural obstacles down there, despite Rich's assurance that the hole's walls had not changed at all. He was also adamant about not returning until he had reached the bottom, and had a variety of tools within his backpack to facilitate such an adventure.

There was a moment of tension as Quinn considered his options, while under the scrutinising eye of the Anton Court residents. He looked over at Crendon, now the de facto face of HP Properties, and silently asked the question.

Crendon just shrugged.

"Fuck it."

With that, Quinn tapped away on his laptop and adjusted the controls of the cable. Soon enough, it stopped unspooling and creaked as it began turning in the other direction. From his position on screen, Rich was bargaining to keep descending, but Quinn had made his choice. While the bigwigs had said it was OK for Rich to go down there, and the wealthy businessman was more than willing, Quinn was still a professional who adhered to a set of rules.

And so, as the sun began to set over Anton Court, from his vantage point below the surface, Rich saw the hole in which he had leapt down grow larger in size. While disappointed, he wasn't angry, and seemed to be ruminating on his next move upon resurfacing.

As for Hannah, she just wanted to be done with the whole thing. While William and Crendon had their own interest in what was happening, as well as The Colonel back in the sanctuary of his home, she had better concerns to attend to.

Specifically, her children.

"When can we come home?"

Hearing such a question from your youngest child was more painful than Hannah expected. It wasn't just the words, it was the innocent tone, the slight whine in inflection that shivered into her ears, and coursed coldly down her spine. Listening to such unfiltered sadness, Hannah made herself swallow to keep herself from breaking, only managing to answer in a single, weak whisper.

"Soon."

"But how soon? It's boring here, and Jarelle keeps taking me in the deep end of the pool. I don't like the deep end!"

This sort of sibling roughhousing brought a smile to Hannah's face. Not that it made the whole ordeal easier, but it was just nice to imagine the two boys mucking around as normal. The sun rose, they lived their normal lives, and then they went to bed to let it all begin again in the morning.

Hannah missed that routine. Part of her needed that routine.

Instead, she was here in Anton Court, a spectator to the ever-increasing debacle that was The Great Hole in the Garden. People shouted at people, rich wankers jumped down and climbed out, and those in charge denied anything bad was happening.

Keep Calm, and Carry the Fuck On.

Hannah wished Greg were there.

Greg always knew what to do. Hannah wasn't the chauvinist ideal of the loyal, meek housewife, but Greg had a knack of making sure that she didn't break. That she always remained firm, calm, and in charge. In control.

Since he passed, she had lost that control. Lost that sense of balance.

She never even got to see the body. Just an urgent phone call, a solemn message from the doctor, and a closed casket. No body, no husband, no father. Just what was left in a box that barely seemed big enough for him.

They said it was a car crash. In her defiance, Hannah demanded to see the car. At the time she really wished she hadn't, but now she looked back and felt it gave her at least a little bit of closure. Truth be told, she knew that by seeing the car, she definitely didn't want to see Greg's body. It wasn't even a car anymore, just a twisted mess of steel and mechanics that looked like it had been chewed and vomited up by some great monster.

And telling the boys... Hannah never wanted to do that again.

Which made being apart from them even worse.

Tim and Louise were doing a great job of looking after them, though. Their spirits were constantly high, and when the parental unit of the Coopers became too much, they could just play with Samantha. On top of that, if the boring life of a child began to drone, then Uncle Charlie would join in and entertain them with his stories. Hannah told him to keep them relatively PG, but wasn't entirely convinced by Charles's attempts at a reassuring smile.

Hannah's role wasn't simply one-way, however. While she enjoyed reconnecting with Jarelle and Warren over the phone, it came with a price. Not a huge one, and not one she despised paying. In fact, it was one that she knew she'd have to pay each time.

The latest gossip from Anton Court.

Of course, the breaking news was Rich's aborted descent. It provoked the odd gasp from Louise, with Tim making sure to question the Health and Safety behind such jaunts.

"It's Rich," Hannah said. "What else do you expect?"

In fact, the whole gossip was pretty standard. Rich dived down the hole, The Colonel complained about the hole, and the rest of the players were the audience.

"With Willy playing professor, no doubt?" Charles said.

"You know it."

In fact, William had begun to take an active role once Rich was abruptly brought back up by Quinn. As the wannabe adventurer sulked and cried about having to come back, William had taken the chance to inspect the hole a bit closer, and also note some residue that had streaked across the cable.

Again, it didn't have the same corrosive effect that Ronnie the Handyman had endured, but it was still intriguing to William. Before her escape home, she had heard him mumble about it being 'minerally'.

"Is that a scientific term?" Tim said.

"It is if he said it," Charles said.

You could see why they were together.

Other than that, nothing more could be said. If they wanted more spice with their chatter, then they could talk to Stacey. For her, the whole thing was far more exciting than it had any right to be. Of course, being Rich's paramour, of course it was. Even his great declaration upon coming out the hole, deftly avoiding Stacey's loving embrace, was far more exciting to her than the others who had heard it.

"What was it?" Louise said, more out of general intrigue than anything else.

"Let me guess," Charles said. "He's named it after himself. The R's Hole!"

Everybody laughed, before Hannah passed on the last titbit.

"Just something about the hole getting smaller," she said. "But you know what Rich is like."

They did, and thought no more about it as the sun set outside, and beds beckoned.

Given the holes penchant for disrupting sleep, Hannah decided the best way to combat it was to self-medicate. And while her spirit selection was lacking, her desk drawer yielded far better results.

She had been prescribed amitriptyline back when Greg had passed, but had refused to take it on what she told herself was 'moral' grounds. It was more a case of she didn't believe she needed them, and so threw them in a drawer and forgot all about them.

But much like Chekhov's Gun, they had come back in the end.

She sank two tablets with a large glass of water, and settled her head on the pillow to finally get some much-needed sleep. She wasn't just tired in general, she was also tired of the nightmares, tired of the way the hole would just make you feel uncomfortable. It was just a natural gap in the ground, but it emitted something alien. It was that feeling that even the Germans didn't have a word for, but one similar to a TV being on somewhere in the house. Hannah's skin was pocked with goosebumps, and the nerves underneath tensed wildly. It felt very much like an itch she couldn't scratch, which infested her whole body.

Well, tonight, she would rip that feeling apart with a few well-placed medicinal hits. The amitriptyline was designed to help her sleep, and after a few minutes of lying in a frustrated doze, it did the job.

For an hour or two.

Once again, it was a slight tremor that stirred Hannah. Not enough to qualify as an earthquake, or even an attempt at an aftershock, but one that vibrated enough to get your attention. She snorted, felt her senses spin into place, and turned over.

Another rumble shook her bed.

It only lasted a second, but it was enough to make Hannah grind her teeth with anger. She was getting sick of this, and the sooner Rich got to the bottom of the hole and found what was in there, the better. In the meantime, the hole grumbled outside, and Hannah growled in the so-called comfort of her bedroom.

Then the grinding started.

It was mild at first, but after a few seconds it got steadily louder. As Hannah lay in bed, listening despite her weariness, the sound of metal rubbing against... something... burrowed into her. The more she tried to ignore it, the louder it got, until she had no choice but to get out of bed and investigate.

She looked out her window, and toward the hole.

The scraping sound got louder.

Her eyes narrowed as she tried to see what was making the noise, but all she got was the perfect circle of the hole, looking back at her.

The grinding made her teeth itch, and caused every muscle in her body to contract. It was steady now; an angry growl of steel slowly moving, being forcefully pushed or pulled. Hannah wanted to step away and cover her ears, maybe take another tablet, but instead she was drawn to finding out what was making this infernal noise.

She didn't have to wait too long to find out.

Much like the rubble that had been expelled previously, from the hole burst forth a mangled sphere. Twisting lengths of mechanical parts wrapped around each other, and once-flat steel now ruptured into welts and angles. The sphere flew out and rose a few feet off the ground before coming straight down into Hannah's front lawn. As it crashed down, she stepped back from the window, and took another look.

The messy ball of metal, as wide as the hole and packed tight, sat quietly on her lawn.

Around the Court, nobody else stirred.

It drove Hannah mad.

Maybe that was why she threw a gown on. Maybe that was why she stomped downstairs and opened her front door. Maybe that was why she was determined to approach this steel ball that the hole had birthed.

As soon as she did, she wished she hadn't.

Steam spat out from between the few cracks in the wreck. As it puffed out its smoke, a vile smell punctured the air. Hannah felt sick, but couldn't move as she watched the ball crack open like an egg, revealing pistons and torn metal.

Now it was unravelling, she could see what it once was.

It was a car.

It was a car Hannah recognised.

It used to be hers.

Theirs.

Hers and Greg's.

The metallic mess continued to unfurl like a flower in some sort of twisted spring, and as the ripped interiors were exposed, the petrol bled onto the green lawn, and springs popped up, something else moved within.

Hannah was no longer angry. She was scared. Her nerves were retching under her skin. Her brain was screaming obscenities at her.

But she did not move.

She did not know why.

Something else moved, though.

And it was as violently mutilated as the car.

A single arm, wrapped in flayed flesh and cloth, clawed at the ground. Every time it threw itself up and landed with a thud, the fingers gripped and pulled.

Behind it, barely attached by the shoulder, were the remnants of a torso. Atop of that, what used to be a head.

Used to be.

But Hannah didn't need all the details to know who it belonged to. Even though it was crushed into a shape not seen in this world, with features thrown around by impossible physics, the eyes rolled around toward Hannah, and a wrecked maw seemed to smile.

Before she heard the words 'Hay-Bay', Hannah screamed.

She was still in bed.

There was no wreckage outside.

There were just sheets, sodden with piss.

While the hole sat peacefully.

Hannah didn't sleep that night.

She cried instead.

Day 6

When Hannah stepped into Anton Court the next morning, there was already a small gathering of the residents. William had taken a seat beside the operations, and Hannah could see The Colonel watching on from his window. Meanwhile, Rich was eagerly getting himself ready with Quinn, while Stacey watched like the loving partner she pretended to be.

At least, until she saw Hannah.

"You look knackered," she said, with the subtlety of a sledgehammer.

Hannah just smiled.

"Looks like you'll need another coffee!"

It was Hannah's fifth that morning.

"Are you ready for Rich to go down?"

The way Stacey chuckled at her own innuendo made Hannah want to smash her coffee cup right in those finely-sculpted cheeks of hers, watching the hot coffee melt every ounce of makeup that had been heavily applied over each curve and contour.

Instead, Hannah smiled far too much, and wandered away.

She made a casual nod of greetings at William, but he was far too interested in what Rich and Quinn were doing. She could tell it wasn't the physicality or sense of adventure that intrigued him, more the overall operation. He was now armed with a wire-bound pad and taking several notes, along with some complex diagrams that Hannah snatched a look at as she walked. She would have enquired more, but she had other things on her mind.

As she approached the Stanley residence, she wasn't expecting to be greeted upon setting foot on their front path. Before she even got anywhere close to their doorbell, the front door opened, and The Colonel was silhouetted against the morning light shining from their back door. For a moment, no words were said, but the tension spoke volumes.

"What would you like, Mrs Suggs?" The Colonel eventually said.

Hannah decided not to correct him.

"How's Heather?"

"Asleep."

Hannah nodded. She could do monosyllabic as well. Better than the old man could, as well.

"Lie in?"

"She didn't sleep well. Doesn't these days. You understand?"

Hannah did. She wondered how The Colonel knew that, though.

"As long as she is OK."

"By which you mean?"

Hannah smiled.

"Just being a friendly neighbour," she said, calmly sipping her brew.

The Colonel studied her for a minute, in a way she'd seen psychologists try to do many times in her past. To be fair, if he'd asked her, she wouldn't have given much more of an answer. The only thing she could really say was that she saw the Stanley's light on in the early hours, and wanted to see if they had been blessed with similar terrors.

But if that meant going through The Colonel... well, it was far too much trouble and even more effort.

Besides, he *did* look tired.

"Not thinking of resting yourself?" she said, acting out a yawn.

The Colonel stifled a reaction, and then made eyes at the spelunking operation currently being prepared. "I think you know as well as I do the... *interesting...* events unfolding."

"It's quite the show."

"Isn't it just," The Colonel said. "Therefore, if you'll excuse me…"

"Not coming to join us?"

The Colonel smiled. Hannah didn't like it.

"I can see very well from here."

Hannah shrugged, and then gave a half-hearted salute.

The Colonel didn't return it.

"I must say," he said, "I'm surprised."

Hannah didn't expect this.

"Surprised?"

"You're not with the boys. Young lads like them, could do with their mother in times like these."

The comment felt like a low blow, and one that hadn't been made in error. Hannah repressed any sort of emotion that The Colonel was trying to pursue, and instead arched her back and scowled.

"They're strong enough," she said. "They take after their father."

"Ah yes, Gregory. A fine fellow. A tragic loss."

"What would you know?"

The tension was easing into the aggressive now, as The Colonel dropped any pretence of politeness and stood firm. In that moment, Hannah realised just how much taller he was than her. His eyes had turned a nasty shade of dark, and for a moment, Hannah felt very scared of the old man.

Because there was no longer a retired military man, there was a Solider, ready to go to war.

"I know more than you'll ever know about loss, Mrs Suggs…"

"*Miss…*"

To her surprise, this seemed to rattle The Colonel.

"My apologies… Either way, I've had experiences you could only know of through your horror movies. You'd do well to respect that now you're aware of it."

Hannah wanted to fire something back about respect, but instead she just stood and watched as the door to the Stanley residence began to close.

But instead of a firm slam, The Colonel was halted from his dramatic exit.

"Mr Stanley, Miss Suggs, if I could have you over here?"

The call came from Crendon, armed with a clipboard in hand and a look of weary determination about his person. Neither party wanted to respond to his beckoning, but then again, they felt they had no choice.

Mostly due to their own curiosity.

But also, mostly due to what they were about to learn.

"Can this wait, Vinnie? I've got a hole to explore," Rich said.

Crendon looked down the hole, and looked back at a trussed up Rich.

"The hole can wait."

"But…"

"The hole. Can wait."

Crendon meant business. He was a firm figure at the best of times, but at the moment he looked like a teacher about to issue out orders to a bunch of children he knew he had no control over.

With the attention of those present, Crendon looked over the board in front of him, sniffed, and got ready to read.

"My superiors have asked me to speak to you on their behalf," he said, sighing as he did so.

Already, hackles were raised, and the residents were ready to strike back at whatever HP Properties had issued Crendon to say.

"As you all know, this... hole, has caused some grievances for you all. Both physically, and... mentally."

There was a knowing glance between the residents. That was enough confirmation for Hannah to know she wasn't the only one blessed with night terrors.

"Well, after putting forward an offer for you to stay at the Garry Hotel – an offer few of you took – HP Properties would now like to remind you of what refusing that offer actually entailed."

This didn't sound good to Hannah. She thought back to her encounter with Norris and whether that had instigated this new memo.

"By staying here," Crendon continued, "you waive all liability on HP Properties for anything that may occur during the period of time the hole is present."

Murmurs rippled through the residents, with only Rich and Quinn not bothered by the statement.

"Your continued presence will mean that any injury, mental or physical, is not the fault of HP Properties. That you are aware of the risks involved with staying in an environment such as this, and that by remaining on site is a non-verbal agreement that you are happy with everything that has happened so far."

"This is ridiculous," The Colonel said.

Crendon tried to reassure him, but decided he couldn't actually be bothered to try.

"You don't like it, you know what to do."

"Leave?" Hannah said.

"If you want. But at this stage... it's permanent."

Suddenly, Hannah found that her hands were being forced.

It only strengthened her resolve.

"I must say," William said, "this doesn't sound very legal to me."

"Feel free to read it, you'll all have got an email."

And that, they say, was that. Crendon threw the clipboard under his arm, and walked away, shaking his head at the position he'd been put in. He didn't like being the bearer of bad news, but every day that this hole was present, he was being plunged further into a shit situation by HP Properties.

Of course, it wouldn't be them that had to answer the questions, it was him. And he was damned if he had the answers.

Then again, no questions came. No arguments arose, and no people stepped forward to challenge the whole damn thing. Hannah, William, and The Colonel just stood there, contemplating this latest move by their 'landlords', and seethed silently.

Each had their reasons for staying. Each had secrets preventing them from leaving. Be it pride, intrigue, or just plain stubbornness.

The only household who were willingly staying stood around the damned hole in skittish excitement.

Finally, Rich was ready to really investigate the hole. His clothing was more appropriate, his backpack fuller, and Quinn looking more pleased by the various straps and buckles that kept his client secure.

The hole was inviting him in, but Rich needed to do one last thing before his final descent...

There was an element to Rich that reminded Hannah of when her kids started school. That nervous excitement that bristled beneath an awkward uniform, worn for the first time, complete with a smile that was eager to embrace the unknown.

As they all stood looking at him, he puffed his chest out and beamed.

"I said before I wasn't going to come back until I reached the bottom of the hole..."

"Which lasted long," The Colonel said, eliciting a surprised, yet suppressed, giggle from Hannah.

"Yes, well, today I mean it! There's no going back. No giving up. I keep descending until I hit rock bottom."

Hannah wanted to tell him he already had.

Unfortunately, people like Rich seem to attract sycophants. Quinn – now sated with the new level of health and safety - was once again excited by the so-called 'coolness' of it all, and Stacey was just in awe of her strapping man, going on a manly adventure. It was more a farce than an expedition, and not helped by Crendon's complete apathy. Hannah looked over at the caretaker, and saw someone not concerned with the safety of those he had been tasked to assist, but now following the orders of his superiors.

Someone should have said something.

But nobody really cared anymore.

Instead, once again, they sat back and watched as Rich dived in, eager to get as far down as possible over the next few hours. He had begged Quinn to let him go down faster, but the more experienced adrenaline junkie remained steadfast in his concern over breaking Rich's back with such a reckless endeavour. It was surprising, given his usual devil-may-care attitude, but Hannah could only theorise that something had happened in his past to inform such a decision.

Of course, such theories didn't matter in the grand scheme of things. All that mattered now was watching Rich fall down, and enjoying the show. William was already ready and waiting, keeping a close eye on the monitor, keeping his own excitement behind a well-rehearsed wall of professional stoicism.

No matter how professional people wanted to be, though, Hannah knew they always got giddy over something like this.

True to his word, The Colonel returned to his home. He had his plan, wished everyone a good day with the same sincere cadence as he usually did, and left them all there to watch.

Hannah had begun to come round to that way of thinking; her bed was calling her to come get some rest, in spite of the ferocious amount of caffeine she had imbibed so far. At this point, sleep was a lost dream, and her new existence was false energy and, of course, the hole.

It was going to be a long day.

After two hours, Rich had gotten nowhere really fast.

He had rappelled just over half a mile, which was impressive to those not in the know, but not good enough for someone of his ambition. He kept begging Quinn to quicken the cable, but to no avail.

"I don't care about injury, I care about getting down."

"That's what the last fella said. Next thing you know..."

With that, Quinn simply snapped his fingers.

In truth, to those watching, it had been a boring couple of hours. Aside from the odd plea, the only other slice of entertainment Rich could provide was the type of inane banter everyone on Anton Court had learnt to tune out. The view on-screen just produced black walls and the odd unflattering illumination of Rich's face, that even Stacey baulked at seeing. It was only the hope that something, anything, would happen that kept the likes of Hannah and William there.

But nothing did.

Nothing too exciting, anyway.

The only thing that tantalised was the structure of the hole's interior. William was keeping a close eye on the camera feed, making notes on what he saw and scraping the odd sketch upon his notebook. When Hannah caught a brief glimpse, all she could make out were words born out of another time, and equations to formula she'd never been taught in college. Science wasn't her thing, but she knew her way around a textbook.

What William was writing was like nothing out of any textbook she'd seen.

In the meantime, Stacey had retrieved some snacks, and they'd all watched as Rich showed off by performing an elaborate routine in order to get a sip of water. As much as Quinn supported his mate, Hannah noticed how much he grimaced at Rich's showmanship. Maybe it was jealousy, maybe it was pride in what he did, but you could tell Quinn didn't like being topside.

After another hour, the first real interesting thing occurred. Rich had already spoken about how the hole was getting tighter, but now that he was a mile underground, he was ready to prove it.

"When I left, I could stretch right out," he said, showing off his six foot physique in vertical form. "But now…"

Rich went to lay out flat at the end of the rope, and sure enough, his head was now scraping the wall. Not just that, but it made his neck bend at a certain angle. Like when you're too high on a pillow, or sat badly on a chair.

It intrigued William, who started to scribble down some more notes, but to the rest of them it was just a hole, which happened to get smaller the further you went down it. Rich went on about his theory of it turning into an inverted cone, while Quinn argued that most caverns stretch out. After all, usually something would burrow up from below rather than down from above.

"Unless someone dug it, you knob," Rich said.

There was a brief murmur from William, who had paused his thoughts at this comment. Hannah waited to see what he would eventually say, but instead he lowered his pen, returned to his notes, and remained silent.

Another hour passed, and Rich kept showing off how the hole was closing in. He pushed his feet against the wall, and smiled as he cramped himself against his surroundings. Hannah looked over William's notes, and saw how he had constructed a drawing of Rich's cone theory, showing how eventually it would taper off.

That would take another 4 miles of cable, which was exactly how much Quinn had left on the back of his truck.

Hannah debated whether she could be bothered to stick around for that long.

In the end, she couldn't, and went back into the house to have a shower.

As the last of the water dribbled out the showerhead, and towels had been strategically applied to the relevant areas, Hannah stepped out of her bathroom and looked outside her bedroom window. She didn't know what she was expecting to see, maybe a fountain of oil with the likes of Rich, Quinn, and Stacey performing a dance ritual under it. Maybe some prehistoric bug crawling out, causing William to jot down some more notes while it devoured The Colonel.

Or maybe, just maybe, Crendon finally cracking and throwing them all down there, to be fed to some sort of Eldritch abomination heralded by him and his employers.

Instead, what she saw was the same banal image as before. Quinn watched the monitors, Stacey watched Quinn, and William watched the hole. In the meantime, everyone else – mainly Crendon and The Colonel – watched on from their respective sentries at home.

The business with the hole had reached a point of utter dullness that it defied reasonable logic to be so invested in it. While it was true that, thanks to the latest doctrine laid down by HP Properties, she was now a prisoner in the very home she was so keen to defend, it was the intrigue around the hole that had really held her there.

Even the nightmares hadn't swayed her from the thought of leaving. As enticing as it was to just leave Anton Court forever, making a home somewhere safer with the boys, she refused to. But the idea that this was out of some form of personal defiance toward HP was slowly being eroded by the idea she was somehow addicted to the hole.

In a way, they all were.

Rich was determined to go down it. William was drawn to study it. And Hannah? Well, she didn't know yet why it appealed so much to her. Maybe it was something to do with Greg…

Before that thought could come to life, the doorbell rang.

A panicked attempt to look presentable was thankfully unnecessary when the visitor turned out to be Heather Stanley. Like many women her age, who adopted the housewife persona most of her generation did, she stood armed with a plate full of edible goods and a polite smile.

"I thought you'd like a spot of lunch?" she said.

Hannah very much did like the idea of lunch. Soon enough the two ladies were sat down in the living room, unfurling a variety of picnic-style snacks including various cooked meats, sandwiches, and slices of cake.

The usual small talk rippled through the first few minutes of socialising; talk of the weather, the Court, and any recent events that didn't involve the damn hole outside. Heather was pleasant enough to talk to, but never seemed to go out of her housewife mode. It was as if she had one mental state, and rarely broke out of it.

Or, at least, so Hannah thought.

"I hear you were worried about me?" she said, sipping away at the herbal tea Hannah had offered.

"Oh, uh, well not really worried, just..."

"I told you before, dear. James isn't like that."

"Oh God! I didn't mean... well what it was..."

Heather seemed to take a naughty amusement in seeing the usually strong Hannah get flustered. It was a rare feeling for her to have, and if it was anyone other than Heather, they'd get a brutal stare-down.

As it was, she just chuckled along.

"I haven't been sleeping well lately, that's all. Neither of us have. James suffers from nightmares anyway. It comes with his work. But I've never had them. Until now..."

It didn't surprise Hannah that James had PTSD. Neither did it surprise her that Heather was having nightmares as well.

"I've been having nightmares," she said, mindlessly stirring her coffee while feeling the exhaustion flow through her veins. "Same shit, every night."

"A loved one?"

Hannah didn't answer. If she was honest, she was scared to. Not that it was deeply personal, seeing your late partner crawl out of the hole in a wretched state, but more that Heather was so prescient with her question.

"At first I just thought it was some silly prank played by those boys next door," Heather said, referring to Rich and Quinn. "But, the second night, I found myself getting up and looking out the window. And I heard, from that hole, the sound of my dear Clive."

Hannah didn't know who Clive was. She didn't want to ask.

"James assured me I was simply dreaming when he found me, but it felt so very real. Hearing his voice sing to me, asking me to come join him on his little jaunt.

"But then the next night, he wasn't so chipper. He didn't sing, but pleaded. 'Oh do come, Heather. Do come and help me up.' Once again, James found me before I left the house and put me to bed.

"Lately, though, it's been awful. Absolutely awful. I never thought I'd see Clive again. I never believed I would. Once he was gone, I left the infernal business. But then, the other night... well, there he was."

The room went quiet as Heather sat there, eyes fixed to the half-eaten crusts and old bones.

"Next to the hole. Seems like Clive had got out without my help. But, Hannah, oh dear. He looked so ill. So very, very ill. I wanted to climb out the window to him. Rush out the door and throw a blanket around his shoulders. His skin was so pale, and his eyes... oh his eyes, Hannah.

"Next thing I knew, James had hold of me and I was almost screaming. It was madness. He told me how hysterical I was and, let me tell you, dear girl, I've never seen him so scared. I know how you all think he's some raging rogue, but in that moment he looked as old as time, and as scared as a youth.

"Since then he's been sat at the door every night, and every night it's the same thing. I want to go out, I want to help Clive, and I want to make sure he's alright."

Heather looked up at Hannah, and met her enrapt eyes with ones stained by tears.

"Because he's not alright, Hannah. He's not alright. He'd dead. He died a long time ago. And I never got to see him until now. I was just told by James. He was dead, he was buried, and that was the end of that. But when I saw him..."

She wanted to go to him. Hannah knew that feeling all too well.

"Anyway," Heather said, "how are you finding the cake?"

It was amazing to think that Rich was now two miles down the hole.

Eager to see more of how far this pit went, he had persuaded Quinn to speed up the cable, and had dropped more than 2 kilometres in the last hour. Despite this frightening level of descent, he had kept informing those up top that the hole was still shrinking in terms of width, and by now he was in a seated position rather than stretched out in a horizontal stance.

Wandering out with Heather, Hannah could see that things had veered pretty far from fun for those above ground. While she was eager to join the group, Heather herself didn't stick around, instead offering a polite wave before retreating to her home.

Near the hole, Quinn watched the screen with professional concern, mostly ignoring Rich's droning commentary and concentrating more on the practicalities of his caving. Stacey was maintaining the aura of Concerned Partner, but now her hand moved more to her mobile phone and other distractions. Hannah wouldn't have been surprised if she was arranging a booty call somewhere to take advantage of Rich being down the hole.

As for William, he was still making notes. His pen scribbled fast over the pad he had acquired, and many pages were now filled with a variety of notes and numbers that didn't seem to correspond with anything Hannah had ever seen. She attempted to get a closer look, but found William's response terser than normal.

"Are you well, Hannah?"

"Just had lunch with Heather."

"Excellent," he said, more distracted than interested. His subtle movement to keep the notes to himself told Hannah all she needed to know.

The only other matter of interest was that The Colonel was no longer hidden behind his net curtains. Instead, he now stood far enough away to not seem interested, but with a focus that betrayed how engaged in the whole process he was. There were no arguments with Crendon, who milled about like a ghost, and no attempts to put forward his usual brash manner. Instead, he stood there, arms folded, and watched. And waited.

For what, Hannah had no idea. Maybe he was psychically prompting the cable to snap and for Rich to descend faster than he had any intention to.

Once again, there didn't seem to be any form of excitement amongst the crowd. Even though they were sharing their own personal event, the residents of Anton Court were just soaking it all in rather than inviting relatives around and milking the occasion for what it was worth. Hannah couldn't help thinking to herself that a person like Rich would have invited all his friends on social media to see what was happening, and that the crowd would be more than a handful of his neighbours.

In the same thought, she wondered if this was a caveat placed by HP Properties. Go ahead and go down the hole, but it is something that is between you, them, and anyone who hasn't gone to the Garry Hotel.

Hannah wondered how they all were. Any form of jealousy was replaced by a lingering sense that while they were safe, they were missing out on something. There was a tiny mental argument telling Hannah to get her kids back, and have them watch Rich on his adventure, but it was a thought that went against every other feeling inside her. A nagging demon prodding away, playing the evil advocate to common sense.

Before she could think more about this oxymoronic ideology, a moment of activity stirred the Court residents.

"Light's going again," Quinn said. "I think we should stop the reel."

"Why? I'm fine," Rich said, his voice crackling from the laptop.

"The less light there is, the more risk. I know you've paid me…"

"A lot, Quinn. And that is to simply supervise my descent."

Everyone could see Quinn fighting with himself over what was happening. It was mutually agreed that Rich would continue down the hole, but the fact they were still to reach anything resembling an end complicated matters.

"I just think..."

"That it's too dark?" Rich said, laughing. As he did so, he spun his camera to look up. Outside of the bare beam of light that accompanied him on his journey, there was nothing but the darkness sucking up any spare illumination.

"I think I can handle dark, Quinn."

There was to be no arguments. When it came to moments like this, a person of Rich's attitude would not budge from his position. And if he was forced to make adjustments, he'd just throw money at the problem. He already had with Quinn, but didn't seem keen on doing it again.

Nevertheless, there really was nothing more to be said. While the sun was beginning to set, and the cable reel that helped Rich with his descent down the hole continued to unspool slowly, everything had reached the point of no return. Whatever health and safety concerns Quinn had, were to be kept to himself.

As the debate petered out and Quinn continued to watch the reel feed into the hole, Hannah looked over and saw someone else finding amusement in the scene before them.

Crendon.

"Enjoying the show?"

Crendon grinned at Hannah's question. "It's just nice to cede responsibility for once..."

Hannah waited for the follow-up comment.

"And to see someone else be pissed off with it."

The two of them laughed as the light of day began to trickle beyond the rooftops of Anton Court. As the sky turned grim, so too did the air acquire a snap. The slight breeze brushed past those standing outside, watching the strange adventure before them, and pricked chills into their skin. As Hannah let out an involuntary shiver, Crendon reached into his jacket and produced a hip flask.

Without saying a word, Hannah took it, swigged the contents, and gave it back with an obvious grimace.

"Lighter fluid?"

"Budget whiskey," Crendon said. "Only the best for me, Hannah."

The monotony of the scene taking central stage in Anton Court was now losing the attention of those who remained there. William had gone back to his home in order to look over the notes he had made, while The Colonel had vanished behind the sanctuary of his curtains. Aside from Hannah and Crendon, the only other audience member still watching was Stacey.

As for Quinn, he just stood next to his laptop, listening to Rich drone on and noting the length of cable that had been fed to the hole.

And Rich didn't stop talking. He continued to inform that the hole was getting tighter the lower he was going, and that the faint illumination from his torch was the only light he now had. The incessant reports didn't just revolve around his conditions, though, but also his thoughts on his adventure, the fame he would no doubt gain from it, and to the interest of nobody, when he relieved himself off camera.

If there was something down the hole, it wasn't going to be pleased with the golden shower Rich was providing.

Hannah and Crendon were amusing themselves in Quinn's plight of having to listen to this drivel and respond accordingly. Luckily, the camera was only one way, so Rich couldn't see his spelunking comrade slouch with weary eyes next to the laptop, giving the odd bored grunt of agreement whenever the time was right. In a way, this whole thing had somehow removed the threat of the hole, turning it into a farce based around Rich's folly. Hannah suggested that would be what they should name the hole, until she noticed someone less amused by the situation.

Stacey had remained steadfast in her refusal to leave the scene of Rich's great descent. She had changed her clothes, yes, but any sense that she would leave to visit one of her 'friends' seemed unlikely. Instead, she gravitated toward Hannah and Crendon, trying to incorporate herself silently into their little group. Hannah always felt like Stacey got a social need from her, desperate to connect with someone other than her wealthy boyfriend on the Court. She was the closest to Stacey's age, and wasn't as motherly as Louise was, so Hannah was the perfect target for Stacey to ease her loneliness.

While this was sad, Hannah always dreaded what inane tattle would come out of Stacey's mouth. As the young woman finally arrived close enough to feel part of the small gathering, Hannah was surprised by what she said.

"I know what you think of me."

Much like Heather before, Hannah found herself stunned and on the defensive. There were no stutters this time, just an awkward silence to be filled by Stacey's cutting words. She correctly guessed that Hannah saw her as a bit of a slut, who was only with Rich for his money, and gave the impression that she lived the life of a stereotypical blonde with vigour.

The truth, she assured her, was somewhat different.

"Men like Rich like to think they have some sort of power, some sort of dominance," she said, watching the cable slowly trickle down the hole.

"I've seen him around girls who question him. You know, challenge him? He hates it. Makes him feel small."

Hannah felt a bit offended. Rich flirted with her, and she felt strong enough. But Stacey soon pointed out that this was a weird form of respect.

"He knows you'll never give in to his so-called 'charms', so he can say the stupid things he does. Bless him. Makes him feel good. I'll admit, there's times when we've been fucking and he's said your name."

"That must make you feel pretty good."

"You don't know the situation," she said, with a grin that said more than Hannah wanted to know.

In the end, what happened behind closed doors told a different story. Like any man who flaunts his wealth and talks too much, Stacey painted Rich as a wounded little boy. A man-child who wanted to feel big and strong, but at the same time needed a mother figure to look after him. To make him feel wanted. To make him...

Well, Hannah didn't want to know what Oedipal issues Rich had.

In the end, Stacey filled her role because of the benefits. The credit cards, armed with infinite limits. The freedom to not just be Rich's concubine, but go out and be whoever she wanted to be, and whoever she wanted to be with.

"In the end, it's a mutually exclusive deal. He fucks about, and I get the money and freedom."

"What if he gets bored?"

"He won't," Stacey said, smiling confidently. "I know too much."

And with that, she wished Hannah farewell with a faint smile, and took her leave.

As for Hannah, she just stood there shaking her head. Apparently, all it took for the secrets of the Court to come out was a bloody big crater in the ground.

She wouldn't be surprised if Crendon admitted he was a serial killer next.

"How many people have you murdered, Crendon?"

"What the fuck?"

It turned out Crendon wasn't a serial killer, just a man who liked his whisky and was willing to share it with Hannah. Without the albatross of assisting the community around his neck, Crendon was actually beginning to show signs of a personality. It was snarky, pleasantly bitter, and made Hannah take a bit of a shine to him.

Then the image of Greg came to her, and all such thoughts were swiftly killed.

Still, Crendon made good company, especially while Charles was back at the Garry Hotel. As the two of them watched the thrilling image of Quinn watching Rich on the monitor, the need to insert their own acerbic brand of commentary was too good to resist.

"What do you think he'll find down there?" Hannah said.

"My will to live?" Crendon said, giving a dark chuckle.

Hannah replied with one of her own, before looking up at the sky. The first few drops of rainfall had just threatened, and with it brought an intriguing dilemma for Rich's adventure.

"If it rains, won't he…"

"Drown? Let's hope so. Might shut him up for once."

"Are you sure you're not a serial killer, Crendon?"

He didn't answer, but the arch of his eyebrow allowed for some comedic ambiguity.

"I've got a canopy I can set up over the hole. The whole area really."

"Sounds like HP have thought of everything…"

"You have no idea," Crendon said.

Hannah took the flask from his hand and looked at him.

"So tell me," she said. "Better the devil you know…"

Crendon didn't respond straight away. Instead, the two of them listened as Rich reported feeling the first spots of rain, as well as his plans to apply a hammock between the walls of the hole. The temperature down there was still clement enough to be comfortable, he said, but the walls were slowly closing in.

"HP are an interesting bunch," Crendon finally said. "Hired me through an anonymous listing. You know, one of those where they don't tell you who they are or what they do."

"Very mysterious."

"Yeah, well, they paid well. Just had to not ask questions. Easy enough."

The two listened to Rich bicker with Quinn over the safety of the cable speed. The rain continued to flicker tiny droplets, suggesting that after this slight calm, a storm was brewing.

"You know why they don't want you here," Crendon said.

This comment snapped up Hannah's attention, and she looked at Crendon as he watched on, not betraying a hint of emotion.

"That hole. This whole development was to get *that* hole. I mean, they haven't said that out loud, but the amount of importance they put on it… they don't care about the houses, you lot, anything but that fucking hole."

"What's so special about it?" Hannah said, recalling Perry's warning from before.

"Fucked if I know. Just that they were more than pissed that I didn't tell them about it sooner, and that they practically wet themselves when they learned that Davis there wanted to go down it."

As Quinn firmly informed Rich the cable would have to be stopped overnight, Hannah felt nervous asking her next question.

"Do they know what's down there?"

Crendon didn't answer.

"Do they know what caused it?"

Again, the caretaker's silence spoke volumes. He threw back the final drops from his flask, and with closed eyes let the rain hit his face.

"They know a lot of things, Hannah," Crendon said, "but I'll be damned if they'll tell me. Put it this way…"

He nodded as Quinn motioned for the canopy to be set up, and sighed toward a slowly dampening Hannah.

"Whatever's down that hole, or whatever made it, is important enough for them to keep a close eye on it, and dangerous enough for them not to go near it yet."

With that, Crendon walked over to his shed to get the canopy, and for Hannah to look back at the hole.

On the laptop monitor, Rich was smiling, enjoying his adventure.

Hannah felt that he wouldn't leave the hole smiling.

Day 7

The next morning, Hannah had to wonder if the hangover was worth it. In the end, such a line of questioning would only end up leading her further down a shame spiral, and she couldn't be bothered with such things.

After all, there was the pure unbridled joy of finally enjoying a night's sleep.

As she rolled out of bed, she wandered to the window and looked down at Quinn's festival-style lodgings. The steady drone of his snoring flickered across the dewy air of the early morn, interspersed with a more familiar voice.

Throwing together what was turning into her uniform, she wrapped her dressing gown over her pyjamas and readied herself for the morning chill. Stepping outside and toward the hole, she was pleasantly calmed by how quiet Anton Court was.

Outside of Quinn's snoring and Rich's constant dialogue, of course.

It was the latter that Hannah found herself most intrigued by. She walked over to the laptop where his stream was constantly broadcasting, and found herself looking at the usual bland sight of the hole's black walls. There was only faint light from the torch attached to Rich, and the camera's feed seemed less clear than before. Yet Rich was still there, talking away.

Except, he didn't sound lucid.

It immediately struck Hannah that Rich was talking in his sleep. Even in a state of slumber, the wealthy neighbour couldn't stop talking. At first, she found this amusing. She was also impressed that, in spite of being nearly four miles down a hole and on what was likely a flimsy hammock, Rich had somehow managed some kip.

But as his words began to form sense in Hannah's ear, her amusement faded.

She'd heard people talk in their sleep before. Jarelle, one night, had sat bolt upright, scaring the hell out of Warren with calm demands for some cartoon-themed notepaper. It was usually just absurdist mutterings, born of a topsy-turvy dreamland where all sense is warped out of logical form.

Only once did she experience the darker side of it. Hannah had heard of people having night terrors, and who verbalised their nightmares in ways that terrified their partners. It had been when Greg had been away on business for a while, and had returned a little bit worse for wear. She'd like to admit that it was due to an obscene amount of drinking, something that she assumed all business people got up to on company jaunts, but there was a haunting nature to Greg sometimes. She would ask if he was OK, trying to get him to open up, but he always told her with a smile that he was fine. During sleep, though, the truth would come out. Greg would start by muttering softly to himself, and then conjure words that made no sense in any form or context. Eventually, he'd scream, sit up, and look around the room in wide-eyed confusion. It took Hannah a good minute to calm him down, with no further incidents occurring afterwards.

As she listened to Rich's soft grumbles, she was taken back to that night. To a time where she had a brief glimpse into a form of fear that went beyond the primal. This wasn't the same fear people have on rollercoasters, or when they see spiders, this was one formed in a mental state that wasn't bound by physical, or even logical, formats.

This was nothing short of insanity.

Much like the whole show of Rich's descent, Hannah couldn't tear herself away from this latest bizarre theatre. She stood there, eyes fixed on the dead screen, but ears listening intently to the speakers. What Rich said didn't make sense; half the time the words weren't even of this language, the rest of the time, they were just inhuman grunts.

But when they did make any kind of sense was when it got disturbing.

Normally, she'd forget such things. She'd shake it off, go back to sleep, and let the mind reset itself in a normal fashion. But what she heard Rich say that morning was enough to stick with her whether she wanted it to or not.

It seemed the payoff to a good night's sleep was to now bear witness to the nightmares of those remaining in Anton Court. Something dark was percolating, slowly coming to a boil and threatening the people in the community. In his subconscious state, Rich was trying to warn her, speaking in fragments that to some would be nothing but verbal mutations. His cadence became alien, and Hannah didn't believe it was Rich that was truly speaking.

"Coming... soon born..."

"Shell is broken... light grows..."

"Too big... must be free... free..."

"Live..."

After this last word, Hannah was thrown backwards in shock as Rich produced a low gurgle that soon erupted into a stifled scream; not loud enough to wake the sleeping Quinn, but audible enough to skewer through Hannah's soul.

As she swiftly made her way back into the safety of her home, she heard Rich make the same confused exclamations Greg had done before. The same confusion, disorientation, and most of all, fear. This time, there was no way she could reach over and convince the person freaking out that they were dreaming, that the nightmares weren't real.

Because this time, the person experiencing this horror was four miles below her, deep down the hole.

It took a while for Hannah to emerge from her home.

The whole saga was starting to make her feel sick, bordering on the insane. She tried retaining a sense of normality by phoning the kids, but their words didn't register and the whole conversation was too cloudy. Hannah then tried speaking to Charles, but he no longer seemed interested in levity.

He was more interested in the hole.

Finally, there was only one person she felt she could talk to.

Perry.

"Morning, Hannah. How are you?"

"I'm going mad," she said.

"In what sense?"

"This hole... I don't know, but it just feels..."

As Hannah spoke out loud, her feelings toward the hole and the situation outside seemed absurd. Not only that, but there were no words to describe why she was scared, obsessed, and ultimately fixated on the hole. Instead, it was something primal that could only be expressed in feeling, something that wasn't physical but was emotional.

She laughed as Perry listened down the other end of the phone.

"It's just a hole, isn't it? Just a bloody hole in the ground?"

"It is a hole," Perry said. "It seems to be affecting you, though."

Again, words seemed impossible to describe everything Hannah felt around her. Language seemed an insufficient tool when it came to the hole dominating Anton Court, and the pop psychologist in her tried to steer her mind away from the more outlandish fears it was conjuring.

Hannah made her apologies and ended the call with Perry, despite the latter's concern. Not even a minute after disconnecting, Perry tried to call back, but Hannah decided it would be a waste of everyone's time. She was being silly, foolish even, thinking that the hole outside was affecting her.

In truth, it was just a hole. While the likes of Rich, William, and HP Properties seemed to hold it in some reverence, she knew it was ultimately nothing. A geographical abnormality, that was all.

One with a power that she couldn't quite place.

Which was ridiculous, of course. It was *just a hole*. Literally, just a hole in the ground. It wasn't a ghost. It wasn't born of any supernatural event. It was just a big hole.

That appeared suddenly.

And had smooth, black walls.

And was over four miles deep.

There was nothing to be afraid of, and that the nightmares were just that, nightmares. The whole thing was just a small-scale hysteria because of how unusual it was. It wasn't the hole; it was Hannah herself that was making her feel like this.

She missed the kids, that was all.

She missed her love.

She missed Greg.

That was the real hole in her life.

She cackled at the blatant metaphor, and finally felt normal again.

After an hour and a couple of strong coffees, Hannah decided to get showered, get changed, and get going. She wouldn't be held hostage any longer by her own mind. She was willing to go to the hotel - HP Properties be damned - and spend time being a mother to her children, rather than a crazy person obsessed with a hole.

Her children were more important than that.

Their children.

God, she missed him so much.

Even as she stood over an empty suitcase, all she could think about was Greg. Words spun around in her head telling her all sorts of debatable truths. Was she an unfit mother? Was his death her fault? Why did she feel all this guilt?

These were the thoughts that the hole conjured, she was sure of it. The living embodiment of her own fractured psyche, fuelling damned lies that did their very best to make sure she knew who was in charge and that she knew her place. It was laughable, putting such a personality onto the bloody hole. It was just her and her own neurosis. Just her, Hannah Suggs, fighting against her own brain as it rebelled against her.

It was nothing to do with the hole.

Still...

Before packing, Hannah decided she had to confront her fears. She had to know if Rich had woken himself from his own personal night terror, if Quinn was watching on for his safety, and if everyone else was fulfilling their bizarre little roles.

Stacey playing concerned little lady.

(*Who wasn't as dumb as she looked.*)

Crendon watching over as site manager.

(*Who knew more about HP Properties than he cared, or feared, to say.*)

William making his notes.

(*Notes that made no sense, to Hannah at least.*)

The Colonel, being The Colonel.

(*Watching, waiting for something.*)

And then there was Hannah herself, the single mother currently without a child to look after. Wanting to go. Wanting to leave Anton Court behind, like a bad memory.

Wanting to get away from the hole.

But before she would, she wanted to find out what was at the bottom of it. What on Earth was so far down, that it was buried five miles under the surface?

Maybe the kids could wait another day.

Hannah had to know what was down there first. Who made it, and why?

If someone, or something, made it at all.

"So what's the latest theory?"

William looked up from his tablet computer to see Hannah standing by. He had set up his little pew again on the lawn adorning the Court's walls, switched from old school paper notes to the new technology, and was currently watching everything with great interest. So much so that when Hannah made her attempt at levity, he was a little startled.

"In the world of science, there is always more than one theory," William said.

"Hence the switch from the notepad?"

William did his best to smile, but made no attempt to disguise his efforts to hide what was on his screen. Hannah did her best to ignore the paranoid demon in her head, and carried on the attempt to be social.

"Anything interesting to share?"

"When I have more data," William said, moving his attention back to the events unfolding at the hole's hub.

Quinn was working away at the laptop, looking back between that and the giant reel on the bed of his truck. Since Hannah's impromptu visit earlier, both he and Rich had woken up sufficiently to begin lowering the millionaire further down the hole. The only real update that had piqued any interest was the fact that Rich's camera was now nothing but a radio; it appeared that the distance he had travelled had gone over the boundaries of the visual signal, and so now the only connection between him and those topside was the sound of his voice. While to the likes of Hannah and William this didn't seem too bad – after all, the view mostly consisted of a dim light shining against a jet-black wall – Quinn took it more seriously. No visuals meant that he was effectively blind, which meant he had difficulty ascertaining the safety of Rich's descent. He was now wholly reliant on Rich's opinion, something that had already tested him many times before.

Still, soon enough Rich's enthusiasm would be limited by his means. Hannah looked over the cable reel and saw that it was beginning to thin out. She had overheard the arriving Crendon mention that only half a mile worth of cable was left. While still a fantastic length, it was a fraction of what was already hanging down the hole.

With Rich dangling on the end like bait.

One thing Hannah sensed as well was that it wasn't just her who wanted to see how this whole spectacle ended. The whole thing had become a private show for the Court residents; a piece of bizarre theatre that beckoned toward an ending they couldn't possibly imagine.

Except Hannah could imagine. Between her nightmares and what she had heard Rich say in his sleep, she had all sorts of horrific visions dancing around in her head.

It was just a shame they were so blurred and vicious to decipher.

This fear was not a lonesome one, though. Looking at William she saw the same concern leaking through his attempts at stoicism. Whatever he was working on wasn't giving him the so-called 'data' he wanted to see. With every tap of his finger and swipe of his thumb, he would sigh heavily and momentarily look quite unsettled, before realising his status and composing himself again.

While Crendon didn't seem to care, and the returning Stacey merely looked on before going to Rich's home to rest, Hannah knew there was one more cautious viewer. From behind his curtains, The Colonel watched on, brow furrowed so deep you could plant seeds in the crease of his forehead.

All this minor tension was all surface level, though. Quite literally. Despite now being a disembodied voice, Rich was still enjoying the thrill of exploring the hole. He advised Quinn that by now the hole had tapered to quite a tight width, meaning he was less abseiling down the hole than walking it, his back pressed against one wall while his feet pushed against the opposite. He had hoped this method would afford him more slack from the cable, but Quinn didn't budge.

Aside from that, Rich had no further peculiarities to report. The climate in the hole was still comfortable, he had been free of any of the corrosive powder that dissolved Ronnie's finger, and he had slept well in his hammock.

Only Hannah made out the slight hint of a lie in his voice.

Still, Rich was keeping up the appearance of an unshaken explorer, talking about how all this would make him famous. Much like Stacey had said to Hannah; while Rich had all the money anyone could ask for, what he really wanted was the adulation.

Which he wasn't currently getting in Anton Court.

"He's still alive, then," The Colonel said, making his way over.

"Seems that way, Colonel," William said.

"And what do your numbers say, hmm? What are the chances of his survival?"

130

William tried to ignore The Colonel, but his presence soon loomed near.

Hannah's attention was now drawn away from the hole, and toward this curious meeting of minds.

"Do your scientific equations tell you what's down there?"

"They tell me what I need to know…"

The Colonel scoffed. "That's the problem with you eggheads. You rely too much on research, not enough on reality."

Hannah was surprised to see William scowl.

"Let me guess. You know what's down there?"

"I know you don't send a civilian to find out."

"Then what was the alternative? You jump down there? Little bit past your prime, aren't you, James?"

It was The Colonel's turn to let his temper show.

"What do you think we're doing here, William?"

Knowing Hannah was present, William declined to answer, turning back to working on his tablet.

"We're watching a man die, is what we're doing," The Colonel said. But instead of containing his usual vitriol, there was an element of sadness to his voice. His eyes no longer blazed with daggers.

"We're all doing what we can do," William said, before looking up at Hannah. "Isn't that right, Miss Suggs?"

The two men now looked on at Hannah, awaiting her input into their mini debate. She silently mouthed a few attempts to respond, before bowing away to Crendon. Whatever strange conflict they were engaging in, she didn't want any part of it.

But even he was lost in a strange fog. As she came over, she saw him quickly pocket some papers with the HP Properties logo on it. Receiving only a polite smile, she found all efforts to engage were met with monosyllables and passive grunts.

Anton Court had turned strange. There was a feeling in the air that a storm was approaching and everybody was preparing themselves accordingly; sharing an unspoken effort to get ready for the worst.

And there was only one place that would happen.

Standing alone, between the tense figures of Crendon, The Colonel, and William, Hannah watched the hole while Quinn stood by it, switching his attention between Rich's communication and the ever-unspooling cable. Something felt off, and it was a feeling Hannah had felt before.

She had often tried to ask Greg about his work. She had offered to act as an ear to bend and shoulder to cry on, but he had always remained upbeat and closed off. On rare occasions he brought his work home, it was always kept safely locked away and duly shredded, and his tech devices were locked down far more securely than you'd expect from a parent of toddlers.

But there had been occasions, much like the one she found herself in now, where a mood descended over him. His eyes would stare a bit further, his teeth clench a bit harder, and as she held him she felt his heart punch violently against his ribs. Any attempt to try and pull out this feeling from him resulted in the same answer.

"It's all good, Hay-Bay."

It wasn't. It was bad, and it had gotten worse ever since they moved to Anton Court. The night terrors. The moments of dread. The secrecy.

Hannah had always assumed Greg did some form of government work, but whatever it was, left him hollow at times.

As she thought about whether her neighbours would be less guarded than her late partner in their fears, something sliced through the tight air.

It was the voice of Rich.

"Whoa! Here we go!"

The words seemed to echo across the Court. Whatever inner turmoil was raging between them all, it was cast aside as the attention moved to where Quinn was listening to the laptop.

"What's up?" he said, leaning toward the laptop's mic.

"It's got pretty tight."

"Can you go any further? Are you trapped? Maybe we should…"

"I'm absolutely fine, Quinn-o," Rich said, chuckling to himself over his friend's panic. "I'm not that fat."

"It's not about fat, it's about danger, you moron."

"I've seen people scurry around crevices thinner than this before."

"Not five fucking miles deep, though."

While a good point, it was a useless one to make. Everyone on the surface were now just playing audience to Rich as he described the claustrophobic conditions he now found himself in. He advised he was no longer walking and had, in fact, not been doing so for a while. Now, he was slinking down the hole straight, feet first.

"Can you move alright?" Quinn said.

"Of course I can! It's like when we cave-dived in Norway…"

Hannah saw the blood drain from Quinn's face.

"Mate, we nearly fucking died in Norway!"

"Exactly! *Nearly*," Rich said from the black of the monitor. "Besides, it's barely scraping my shoulders…"

Rich continued to describe his surroundings. The image he conjured was that of a tube, not dissimilar to the end of a funnel. While his wiry frame could navigate with little difficulty, he suggested anyone of stockier build would soon find themselves wedged in the hole. As he told everyone of his uncomfortable shimmy, Hannah could see that the giant reel of cable was almost at an end.

And then, she saw it stop.

"What happened?" Rich said.

On the grounds of Anton Court, all eyes were now on a very scared Quinn. He had punched the controls to the cable, and stood contemplating his decision.

"I'm calling it, mate."

There was silence from the laptop.

"Rich?"

"How much cable is left?"

"It doesn't matter. I'm calling…"

"1 million."

Hannah's jaw nearly dropped. She knew what Rich was saying, and she saw Quinn react accordingly. If he let Rich continue to descend, against his morals, he'd be an instant millionaire.

Nobody else was amazed as Hannah was, though. Instead, the likes of William and The Colonel just watched on, wanting to see what happened next.

"Wha… what if you die?" Quinn said.

"Then I die a damn hero," Rich said with a laugh. "And you'll still be a million pounds richer. You have my promise. I'm assuming you have witnesses there."

Quinn finally acknowledged the crowd that had surrounded him at his station, and saw that expectation was etched across their faces. Only Hannah was as scared as he was.

But she wouldn't be a million pounds richer for what happened next.

It took a moment of soul-searching, but finally Quinn relented. He reached back at the controls, flicked a switch, and they all listened as the giant reel groaned once more.

Over the laptop, Rich whooped with glee.

William, The Colonel, and Crendon remained emotionless.

Only Hannah felt as sick as Quinn looked.

Now that the severity of the situation was obvious to those above ground, time was largely irrelevant. After all, what was a minute here, an hour there, when all your focus was on a blank screen, and a speaker that was sounding tinnier with each passing moment?

Hannah would have liked to admit that she was above such things. Much like any of the other residents, she would have loved to say that she could have walked away. But much like the grip that kept her within the Court, now she was firmly captivated by Rich's journey down the hole. She stood there, flanked by Stacey, William, and The Colonel, while Quinn crouched next to the speaker, listening intently.

There wasn't even that much to listen to, just the strains of a man trying to get through what was less than a hole now, more of a narrow passage. Rich's progress had slowed, but his determination was at an all time high. With each strain, he made a couple of feet to get ever closer to his goal to reach the bottom of the hole. Of course, this was absolute hearsay; there was nothing to suggest the hole *had* a bottom, and the goal was less defined by Rich's own perseverance, but more the limits of the cable Quinn had provided him with.

Any concerns of his safety were now firmly planted in the back of everyone's mind. It was strange, that they had all finally drank the proverbial Kool-Aid and become the enrapt crowd of Rich's dreams. All eager to see him succeed and become the world-famous explorer of his dreams.

After all, it was hard not to look upon this feat and be impressed; Rich was now lower than any human being had ever been at an impressive five miles below the surface. In truth, he physically shouldn't have been that far underground, having hit impenetrable rock a long time ago. And yet, the hole afforded him an entrance into a world people had only dreamed of, even though all he described were black walls lit by dim light.

Rich hadn't provided much more description. The only new detail he gave was the firmness of the hole's walls. Higher up, they had been solid and with little give. Now he was further down, there was more of a softness to them; a fact he put down to a change in 'rock density'.

While this amused William, what Rich said next culled any levity above ground.

"It's squishy, like going down a throat."

This statement made Hannah shiver.

Any further description was now moot. Rich confirmed that the tightness of the hole, while still giving enough to wriggle lower, did not give much of a view. His commentary turned into a series of struggling grunts, and the slight sound of his body rubbing against the walls of the hole.

Hannah stood there, lost in the thrall of Rich's odyssey. William stood equally entranced, only giving the occasional tap at his computer, while The Colonel was having more difficulty hiding his concern behind his grimace. As for Stacey, she remained a blank canvas, mentally preparing for her future in a myriad of ways.

The only person no longer present was Crendon. He had disappeared while everyone concentrated on Rich.

This bothered Hannah, for reasons she couldn't explain.

However, before she could investigate further, Rich's latest monologue about how he should have a statue erected in his honour suddenly came to an abrupt stop.

All eyes looked toward the laptop monitor that had been broadcasting Rich's descent, and all ears desperately searched for some sort of sound that confirmed he was still alive.

Eventually, they got that confirmation.

"I think I've reached the bottom," Rich said.

At first, the residents of Anton Court, along with Quinn, were shocked. They had begun to believe there was no bottom to the hole, and yet here was Rich, confirming that he had found it.

Until he clarified.

While he had reached the bottom of the hole, he had not reached a surface in which to stand. He described to those listening that his feet were no longer kicking against the walls of the hole, helping pulling him further down, but instead seemed to dangle in the air. He explained to those listening that he was able to kick about freely, while the rest of his body was still constricted by the hole.

With barely contained excitement, he began to shuffle harder down.

A strange excitement began to take hold of those present. Quinn's terror turned into blind joy, smiling so widely it almost looked like his lips were about to split open his cheeks. Stacey couldn't control herself, and was jumping up and down like an epileptic rabbit, cooing at her 'brave man'. Even William couldn't control his astonishment over what Rich was saying.

The only person still remaining as serious as Hannah was The Colonel.

"It's a cavern," Rich said. " Yeah, definitely a cavern. I'm moving my legs below the knees. Nothing there, just space. Loads of space."

He laughed, and Quinn joined in. He even grabbed hold of Stacey and kissed her.

They were the only ones.

Hannah felt bad. Really bad. She couldn't shake that feeling, the infernal one that had been creeping across the back of her head ever since that first nightmare. It stung, like a filthy dressing rotting against a wound, and yet she couldn't cure it. Couldn't itch it. It just kept reminding her it was there, getting worse.

She looked around, and saw The Colonel wasn't far behind.

He did not move. He did not flinch or change his position from standing perfectly still, arms firmly across his chest. And yet his eyes spoke volumes. While William looked interested in what was happening, The Colonel was scared. He would not dare show it, but his face remained a blank canvas only through sheer force. His eyes betrayed him, though. They looked like they were seeing atrocities on a global scale. They roared at Hannah as she looked at him, raging worse than The Colonel had ever done.

Yet he did not move. He did not change his stance.

He just stood there, waiting.

Rich laughed as he kicked his legs about. The cavern was up to his waist now, and he was shuffling the last of his torso down so he could finally see what he had wanted to see since he entered the hole. It wasn't the untouched floor he hoped to stand on, but it was something far more outstanding - a giant cavern, ready and waiting for further exploration.

Nobody said it, but they all knew the cable was coming to an end. Not that it mattered, as Rich raved about how he'd find a platform, something he was sure would *obviously* in the cavern *somewhere*, and he'd get Quinn to send more rope down so he could tie up and carry on.

Even though this plan didn't make sense, Quinn didn't care. He was on board completely, not caring how the rope would go down there or even the safety behind it. The three of them just spoke about how they'd 'throw down' some supplies like it was that easy. Like Rich hadn't just spent over 24 hours getting down the hole in the first place.

No, they were all just too eager to hear more about this cavern, which now housed everything below Rich's chest. He swung on the rope with glee, actually making sounds that reminded Hannah of when Jarelle and Warren first went on a rollercoaster. He was practically giddy, doing his best to describe in detail what he was experiencing.

Unfortunately, all that came out was how amazing it all was.

"It's glorious," Rich said. "It's absolutely glorious. There's such freedom down here, such space. This cavern... when I get the light out, I'll tell you. But it must be... bloody Hell. It must be fucking huge!"

As he had wriggled down, to get through the last few feet, Rich had positioned his arms above his head. Therefore, now he had entered the cavern, the last thing to pop out the holes bottom was his head and his hands. As his shoulders squeezed through the iris, there was one final groan before Rich gasped, and he spoke to those listening.

"I'm here. I'm finally here."

He told them he was hanging by the rope, in a huge expanse of space his camera's light barely lit.

And even though his breath was quick and shallow, he sounded happy.

It would be the last time he was.

There was only one question on everybody's lips.

"What can you see?"

Strangely, it was William who asked the question. He had forced himself between Quinn and Stacey, and was now standing firmly next to the monitor, listening in intensely. As they all looked at him, Hannah thought about how invested he was. Even showing a little fear.

They didn't show it, but they were all scared. After all, Rich had just found some great unknown within the Earth itself; it was hard not to be scared as well as brilliantly impressed. And yet William now just stood there, firing off question after question before Rich could answer any.

"Tell me, what can you see?"

"Who is that?" Rich said.

"It's William Barrett. Now, Richard, tell me what you *see*."

"Well, Billy, would you like to know what I see?"

"Yes."

There was a brief pause.

"Bugger all."

Quinn and Stacey laughed.

William remained serious.

"What's the temperature down there? Is it hot? Cold? What does it smell like? What can you hear?"

"Calm down, Willy, you'll get your interview in due time. Just after the usual big hitters. I'm thinking Time, I'm thinking the BBC."

None of this was impressing William. He looked ready to lose his temper, something that scared Hannah more than the hole did. William was a calm man, one never to show much emotion. Charles was always the emotive one in their marriage, and yet here he was, ready to shout at Rich through the speaker for his arrogance.

Instead, he stepped away, took a breath, and wiped his hand over his face.

All the while, The Colonel looked on.

While Rich continued to brag through the monitor, Hannah checked on William. He looked flushed, exhausted, as if he had just gone through some great trauma.

"Do you need to go inside, get some rest?"

"I'm not leaving."

"Look, I get that. I don't want to leave either, it's just…"

"Hannah," William said, turning and taking her hand. "I'm not leaving. I can't leave."

"It's just going inside."

"He's not leaving."

They both looked over, and The Colonel glared at them.

"He's not leaving, none of us are," he said, eyes slowly moving their glare from Hannah back to the hole. "We're staying until it's over."

"Until *what* is over?"

No answer. The Colonel didn't need to. Hannah knew what he meant.

Just because Rich had reached a cavern, doesn't mean he had reached the bottom.

Instead, William took his seat once again, and watched on. Hannah stayed with him, despite wanting to go over to join Quinn and Stacey as they listened in. At the moment, it was just the hubris of a wannabe adventurer expounding how great he was at, what was essentially, falling down a hole.

Then again, he was down there; they were up here. Maybe his confidence had a point.

"I feel like I should say some important words," Rich said over the monitor.

"Well you can't bloody say one small step for man, can you?"

"I know, already taken."

"No! You ain't stepped on anything yet!"

Quinn and Stacey laughed, and Rich joined them. His voice sounded weak over the monitor, almost broken. Hannah came closer in order to listen in better.

"Let me have a look, see if there's any cliffs or something."

"Cliffs? Down a hole?"

"You know what I mean! There's bound to be something…"

Silence. Just the sound of Rich's breathing. Slowly. Deep in. Hard out. Over, and over again.

And then, he spoke.

"I think I see something."

They all listened.

It was Stacey that spoke.

"What is it, babe?"

"I think… Well, it looks like..."

"What?"

Nothing.

"Rich, what is it?" Quinn said.

"Pull me up."

"What?"

"Pull me up."

"Rich, what's…?"

"*PULL ME THE FUCK UP.*"

The next few hours were torture.

Those who could not help pulling the cable up faster, instead had to listen to Rich's incessant screams through the laptop monitor. He had remained calm at first, albeit breathing fast and heavy whilst mumbling some sort of mantra. However, when it seemed like he couldn't get through the same small aperture he had wriggled down, then the screaming started.

Nobody quite knew how this particular doom was overcome, just that once the cable started pulling Rich back up, assisted by the hands of Quinn, Crendon, and Hannah, he had managed to push himself through. Amidst the maddened screams, the only other sound those topside could hear was a sickening scratch as Rich clambered up the walls of the hole to escape.

The whole nightmare seemed to last forever. Afterwards, as Hannah lay on the ground and let the first drops of rainfall on her face, she wondered how exactly they had done it. The length of cable, five miles of it, pulled up with the type of speed you'd retract a tape measure. Their hands were red raw as they pulled, and tried to block the sound of Rich out of their heads.

If that wasn't enough, Stacey had launched into a horrific panic. She roared at them to pull faster, as if that was some magic formula to get Rich to the surface. Only now did they all realise the reality of how far down he was, how far away from them he had gone.

"Why aren't you helping him?" she'd scream, and Hannah wanted to slap the fear out of her.

Instead, she kept pulling.

As the hole got wider, Rich attempts to climb became more reckless. Instead of getting back up, he was falling back down, prone on the end of a massive reel. Supplies fell from his open backpack; his camera swung around and hit him in the face. Not that Rich felt it; he was too far gone to notice such things.

All he did was weep and wail.

The rain began not long after the whole affair started. Those assisting in bringing Rich back, now including both William and The Colonel, groaned as the cable became slick in their hands, turning their efforts into a farcical tug of war.

Looking back, Hannah smiled hysterically at how the community came together to save one of their own. No matter how much the likes of William and The Colonel did not care for Rich, they still made the effort to help him. At least, that's what Hannah recalled. She couldn't be 100% sure if their efforts were born of altruism or something else.

Several hours. It took so long that even when asked, Hannah could not tell. She just remembered lying on the ground, letting the rain wash over her, and trying to recall when things were normal, when they were simple.

When Quinn finally saw Rich, his silence spoke more than anything else. Nothing was said, nothing was relayed back to the rest of them as they pulled, but they all saw it themselves when he finally emerged.

Covered in his own blood, from where his head and body had smashed against the hole's jet black walls and his now nailless fingers had clawed at them, Rich looked like Death had embraced him and not let go. His skin was pale, sweat mixed in with the crimson, and his whole body shook in an uncontrollable panic.

As soon as he got a grip of the ground, he threw himself up, clambered to his feet, and ran toward his house. His gait was erratic and fragile, causing him to fall several times as Quinn and Stacey chased after him.

The rest of them simply collapsed in exhaustion. It had been a brutal exercise in endurance and adrenaline, and now it was over the only thing left to do was fall themselves. But not toward the hole. Whatever Rich had seen down there was enough to make them all push themselves as far away as possible.

While the rain washed away Hannah's own exhaustion, one final thing about Rich flashed through her head. A silly little thing, but one that made her feel sick.

Upon coming out the hole, he didn't blink.

He didn't blink once.

He just stared, with eyes so wide they seemed to almost fall out of his skull.

And they were scared.

So very scared.

Nothing.

For the next two hours, nothing happened in Anton Court. Every resident just tried getting along with their lives, tried to place recent events into a context where everything made sense, and life was simple once more.

Of course, it wasn't. It never would be. That was the prevalent feeling across the Court. That was the real 'nothing' that was happening; that void of safety, of security, that you once had. That absence of knowing that you had everything figured out, and the world wasn't so scary after all.

Now, it was. Or at least, they all thought it was. No one said it to any other, but they all felt it. Crendon staggered to the sanctuary of his home, and The Colonel shared a venomous exchange of glances with William. It would be obvious to say something had changed, but the way things had changed was unusual. As Quinn and Stacey forced their way into Rich's home – now freshly barricaded as much as he could in that short space of time – Hannah tried to shift her thoughts into neutral.

As she did so, her attention was dragged toward the hole. It was there, as it had been, silent and open.

And even more dangerous.

Time danced in these 2 hours. It hopped around and ceased to work in a normal fashion. Hannah moved in a glide, as life around her melted into a dream world. Her phone rang, the rain slammed against her window, but it was all lost in a fine mist. She undressed, showered, re-dressed and ate some food. She sat on her sofa, the same one she had watched silly films with the kids and Greg, and stared into space. Except, it wasn't just space, it was something.

She just didn't know what.

But that was all she could do. Just sit there and stare. Wait for the next thing to happen, because it *would* happen. Something was bound to. The calm before the storm, the long exhale before the fight. The bitter words shared between William and The Colonel that suggested a knowing darkness. The way The Colonel spat about culpability. The temporary weakness of William looking over his typed notes. Heads and hands shook, ugly and scared.

But such a fear was minor compared to the one being faced by Stacey and Quinn. That fear, one that was wretched and gutting, could be seen as they pleaded and panicked over Rich's state of mind. Watching them try to get inside, and eventually succeeding in spite of countless efforts to block the world out, made your soul hurt. Seeing Stacey crying hysterically, and Quinn locked in a state of shock.

Something would happen, and while it took two hours, it soon did. The quiet that had settled was being disrupted. The air was turning thick, the atmosphere vomiting invisible bile around her.

Hannah couldn't help but throw up herself. As the tap swirled away the empty slithers of sickness down the drain, she saw the world warp outside.

The rain stopped. The clouds parted, and revealed a blood red sky burning into the black of the night.

Hannah's door thudded with a knock twice, and twice again, before she rose up to answer.

It was Quinn.

Nothing was said.

Nothing was done, except to follow him to Rich's house.

Nothing would be the same.

Nothing.

When Hannah and Greg's children were asked what they thought Hell was, they both drew the same picture. A place decorated in fire and smoke, with little imps handling little pitchforks dancing around sad men and women, while a big man with fangs watched over them. At the time, Hannah and Greg laughed at their boys' simplicity when it came to such ideology, and assured them such a place did not exist.

Now, Hannah knew that for sure. Hell wasn't a place where demons danced around scalded bodies for all eternity; it wasn't ruled by a giant Satanic figure who mocked the afflicted and basked in his kingdom of everlasting suffering.

No, Hell was something quite different.

It was here. It was Anton Court.

The air in Rich's house was oppressive. It sat on you as you walked through the door and stepped through its corridors, silently greeting the other residents who had already been summoned by Quinn. He left them to their own words, and Hannah did her best to smile.

147

The command didn't reach her lips. Instead, she just stood there, blank.

Along with William, Crendon, and The Colonel.

Before she could even ask where Heather was, The Colonel just shook his head. She wouldn't come. She'd never come to an occasion like this.

Not after the nightmares she'd been having.

Hell, none of them would have really.

Maybe they were just stronger.

As the lone woman, it was Hannah's plight to feel the wailing limp grasp of Stacey as she entered the room. She sang a chorus of dead chords, drenched in tears that hadn't stopped since Rich had first cried to be rescued. She talked to Hannah, but Hannah heard nothing. She was numb, just another body here to embrace the anarchy, another spectator to the saga of the hole. Stacey couldn't stop herself, she wept and fell to her knees, but no one helped her. No one even moved. They just stood about, waiting for whatever came next.

After this episode, Stacey pulled herself off the floor, her face covered in streaks of makeup that betrayed her attempts at glamour, and desperately tried to put on a brave face. She stretched her lips up in a smile, but the expression didn't hold, and instead she asked them to follow her.

Quinn had gone, not that it mattered. Like them, he was just another puppet in this macabre show. His role was no longer required, and so he had been packed away somewhere to be revealed later. Instead, Stacey led up the stairs, with Hannah behind her, followed by William, Crendon, and The Colonel. Out of all of them, he was probably the most focussed, but that didn't mean he took charge. Instead, he followed them, and kept his surveillance active.

On reflection, one could say that Rich's house was quite decadent. They all shared common structure, but Rich had designed his in a way that it almost felt like a mansion. The corridors stretched for miles, and each room seemed like a cavern in itself. It was painted in stark colours, with the only pictures being of the couple themselves, either in an embrace or flanked by faces that sparked names you'd read about in magazines. In each photo, Rich smiled brightly. He had an expression that was warm, that was proud, that told you he knew how good he was, and wasn't afraid to show it off. They were both dressed in fine clothes, at fine occasions, and projected a life most could only dream of.

They were, in a strange way, stars.

Eventually, all stars went supernova, and now it was Rich's time. Stacey already was no longer the starlet socialite she believed herself to be. She was just another lost little girl, with her mother's make up smeared over her face like a clown, and her firm fashion sense hidden by a jumper and some jogging bottoms.

The tension almost choked Hannah as they reached their destination. Stacey stood at the closed door, and seemed to hold back the emotion she was so open in spilling downstairs. For a good minute, she just stood there, hand on the door handle, rocking back and forth.

It was William who stepped forward, took her hand, and allowed Hannah to open it up.

Stacey burst into tears onto William's shoulder.

The rest of them just went inside.

In normal circumstances, you would call Rich's master bedroom beautiful. As white as the rest of his abode, it was covered in the finest furniture, the classiest silks, and gave a general sense of minimalist tranquillity.

Of course, this was in normal circumstances. In the current circumstances, all of this peace was out the window, thanks to liberal smears of blood that hadn't been as hidden as well as Quinn had done with the rest of the house.

The residents filed in, led by Hannah, and looked over to the bed where Rich lay alone, head stacked against a pile of pillows. His eyes hung in their sockets, covered mostly by droopy lids that suggested a state of artificial calm. He said nothing as they walked in, instead allowing drool to slowly trickle out the corner of his mouth. As Hannah got closer, she saw the pile of pills that had been emptied on his bedside drawer, and then the vomit that had been forced out by Quinn. At this stage, Rich had enough tranquilisers in his system to knock him out.

Not, thankfully, to kill him.

The others filtered around the room, looking at each other in confusion as to what to do or say. William continued to do his best to comfort Stacey, but his mind was elsewhere. In a short moment, Hannah watched his eyes dart between Crendon and The Colonel, with the latter getting more focus.

They stood like statues, glancing over the prone Rich, before any action was taken. It was to be attempted by Crendon, but his deep breath and hesitation allowed The Colonel to swoop in, and take a seat next to Rich. Stacey had moved it there to take Rich's hand, leaving it now limp outside the duvet.

Everyone waited to see what The Colonel would say. He wasn't the most tactful of people in the world, but he had taken it upon himself to interrogate Rich. Hannah wanted to step forward and stop him, but found herself shocked at his calm manner.

"Richard," he said, his voice echoing a smooth lilt rather than the usual vitriol. "Richard, can you hear me?"

"He's quite out of it," Stacey mumbled, but The Colonel took no notice. He kept looking at Rich, waiting for the young man to look back.

After a bit more waiting, and a bit more coaxing, his head finally turned to face The Colonel.

Who then smiled.

Hannah couldn't believe it.

"Richard, how are you?"

A flicker of amusement wafted over Rich, before his stunned grimace returned.

"Been better, no doubt?"

Rich slowly nodded.

"Would you like some water? Maybe something a little stronger, perhaps?"

Rich nodded.

"Water."

Hannah still couldn't believe how soft and how caring The Colonel acted. He slowly offered the glass to Rich, pouring the drink slowly between his lips as Rich tried to lift himself. As the water began to fall down his chin, The Colonel pulled away, and let Rich's head fall onto his pillows.

"Richard, are you OK to answer a few questions?"

Rich nodded.

"Are you sure? It's about what you saw. Down there."

There was a pause. Rich's breathing became a little faster, and Hannah could hear Stacey begin to get hysterical again.

Eventually, it all became calm again.

Thanks to The Colonel.

He took Rich's hand, and gripped it tight. Rich looked up to see the old man smiling at him, warmly, and tears seeped down his cheeks.

Finally, he spoke.

"It doesn't make sense."

It was The Colonel's time to just nod and listen.

"It was... it *has* to be... too big."

No one said anything.

"It... I don't... I don't know..."

"It's OK, Richard. Be calm."

"I mean, nothing... nothing could be that *big*?"

With that, Rich's head rolled to face the other side.

The Colonel, while calm and playing the excellent role of carer, was not finished.

"What makes you say it's 'big'?"

Rich didn't answer at first.

The Colonel gripped his hand tight.

"Please, Richard, for me. Tell me, what was it?"

Rich slowly rolled his head over, and looked at The Colonel.

"Rivers..."

The Colonel nodded, slowly, calmly.

With a smile on his face.

Hannah couldn't tell if he cared, or was just curious.

"Red rivers... like giant veins"

"Veins?"

"It was dark, and then... it moved."

"What moved?"

It was Rich's turn to smile. It looked freakish.

"Its eye. The veins... in its eye," he said, pointing at The Colonel's own eyes. "They were like big red rivers."

Hannah couldn't tell at this point if Rich was laughing or crying. All she knew was that when he started wailing, she wanted to leave.

She wasn't the only one.

There was no other way to put it, Stacey was broken.

While Rich was obviously mentally shattered beyond repair, he also had the blessing of insanity to shield him from the worst. But Stacey was all too aware of the horrors that had swiftly disrupted her life. The efforts made by her and Quinn to prevent Rich from committing suicide left them exhausted, but the emotional torment Stacey endured was the most brutal. Quinn had the beneficial excuse of work to take him out of what was happening, but all Stacey could do was drift around the house like a ghost. Never settling in one room, never taking a moment to pause, just gliding between doors, looking for an end she couldn't find.

And much as she had been before, Hannah was her designated shoulder to cry on, whether she liked it or not.

By now, a second bottle of wine had been opened, and the offer of an extra glass was too much of a gesture for Hannah to politely turn down. She wasn't much of a fan of the grape – whisky being her tipple of choice – but when in Rome...

As Hannah watched Crendon slip outside the front door, Stacey remained silent at the other end of the table. Small talk was off the menu in times like these, and her attempts to ease her restlessness just resulted in Stacey foregoing the glass and rather cleverly dipping a series of conjoined straws down the neck of the bottle.

Hannah began to shift about herself, unsure of what words were required in a situation like this, when the words finally came from Stacey.

"I can't do it."

This was fair enough, given the stress. Then again, Stacey had already gloated about using Rich's money for her own means. Now that the time to actually play Caring Lover was upon her, the heat was a bit too much.

"I know it's cruel, and I know it's wrong, but I can't do it. I can't look after him."

"It's... a tough situation," Hannah said, debating whether she should play Yes Woman or Devil's Advocate.

"Quinn says its just shock, but he gets to go home tomorrow. He gets to drive away and leave this behind him. I've got to clean the sick, wash the blood from the sheets, be a *fucking* housewife..."

Several sentences swirled about around Hannah's mouth, before she decided to just shut up and nod.

Both of them sat in silence for a moment verging on the uncomfortable. The right thing to do, or at least the one thing that sang seductively in Hannah's mind, was to let Stacey stay with her. Give her a respite and let Quinn keep an eye on Rich.

Then again, Hannah couldn't think of anything worse. Yes, Stacey was in a vulnerable place right now, but she was still *Stacey*.

Such casual cruelty made her feel wretched.

Nevertheless, a variation of the offer slipped out between Hannah's lips.

"Is there anything I can do?"

Nothing. Not even a small hint at the possibility of two gals spending a wild night together, gossiping about the boys. Not even a flicker of excitement in her eyes. Just dull pain, resting heavy on Stacey's shoulders, waiting to be taken off.

But it wasn't ready to be taken yet.

"Tomorrow," she said, eventually.

"Tomorrow what?"

"Help me pack, help me get a lift to the nearest station, and help me leave. It's for the best."

"Do you really think…?"

"Hannah," Stacey said, her eyes finally moving from the table. "Please. Just help me, OK?"

It was shock, it had to be. They all just needed to rest, think about what was being said and done, and then in the morning it would all be different. Statements would be retracted, fears shaken off, and promises forgotten.

"I promise," Hannah said.

She didn't even touch her wine.

Instead, she walked from the kitchen, and down the corridor. There was nothing more to be done here, except let the lights go out and hope that sleep would come easy. It was rough, but then, everything seemed to be these days. Long gone were the times when the only stress was from HP Properties.

Hannah wondered what their response to this would be. Surely they'd be aware of their part in Rich's current condition, and take the responsibility accordingly.

As she went to leave, she passed William, standing by a closed door. Except, of course, it wasn't closed; it was just ajar enough for someone to spy into, and William was very closely spying.

He was terrible at hiding his guilt.

"Hannah, I was just…"

"Leaving?" she said, a little smirk on her face.

William took the opportunity, and opened the door to let them both out. The Colonel had long since left as well, and it was time to let the Davis household descend into a nice, quiet calm. Rich was drugged into a stupor in bed, courtesy of his own private supply he'd accumulated over the years, and Stacey was drinking herself to sleep. Meanwhile, Quinn was busy elsewhere…

As Hannah had a sneak peak through the crack herself, he was watching what video footage Rich had managed to get. It was dark, it was messy, and it didn't make a lot of sense.

But then again, Hannah assumed that was just all she could see in that quick glance.

Something like a wave crashing, and turning black waters a chilling white.

Complete with red rivers.

Day 8

There were no nightmares that night. This was the first hint that something was amiss.

In fact, as Hannah slowly came round, the feeling of a good night's rest seemed almost alien. Sleep had taken her as soon as her head had hit the pillow, and with no alarm nor any children to wake her, she had slept in till the wonderful time of 10AM.

As she lay there, covers messily resting over her, she actually felt good for the first time in a long time. She felt rested, relaxed, and ready to take on the day ahead.

Ready to finally get her life back to normal.

Hannah smiled. Even though part of her didn't trust these positive feelings.

She took her time getting up, enjoying this brief respite against the saga of the hole outside. The day before had been intense, and she briefly wondered how Rich was this morning, and whether Stacey had changed her mind about deserting him.

Now she was blessed with a more positive mind-set, Hannah assured herself that everything was fine.

Everything was always fine. Before the hole.

It took half an hour, but eventually Hannah slipped out of bed, washed up in the bathroom, and fixed herself a coffee. The curtains were closed, but the sun outside shone so brightly that they didn't need to be open. In fact, being in a serene dimness suited her drowsy head. She allowed herself to float around the house, chilled out and coasting along without a care in the world.

Even the coffee tasted good. Hannah had seemed to forget about the simple pleasures in life. The sweet bitterness of that first brew, the stillness of the late morning, and the general sense of freshness that comes with waking up. It all felt strangely natural, like a memory that comes back to you, filling you with light.

It was a curious feeling.

She thought again of the days before the hole, before Greg was taken from her. Before the kids. When they were carefree and fancy free, just two young people enjoying their lives. Sitting on the edge of her bed, Hannah remembered those moments. She remembered the times when Greg would return from work for the week, and they'd spend a weekend in bed – if they were really lucky – without a care in the world.

And then, like all good memories that drifted lazily around the mind, one came to Hannah; one where they lay in bed, on a morning like this, and they just looked at each other. Greg would play with her hair, like he did every morning, but did so then with a tenderness she missed. He carefully pushed aside the stray lock that fell between her eyes, and seemed to study each curve of her cheekbones, each bead of sweat that sat carefully on her brow.

In that moment, time stood still, and he told Hannah he loved her for the first time.

Jarelle was conceived that morning.

It seemed like a steady ascent of joyous escalation after that. First came Jarelle, then Warren. They became a family, one completely without a care in the world. There were no messy teething problems, no stern arguments. Sure, Greg worked more and more, but when they spent time together, it was always filled with love.

On rare occasions, they'd have times like these, times similar to this morning. Where life would leave them alone for a brief moment and let them just be. Let them relax and adjust to the world instead of being ripped out of bed and pushed into it. Where they would lay there, playing with each other's hair, and telling each other they loved them.

Peaceful moments.

Beautiful moments.

Calm before the storm.

Hannah finished the last of her coffee, stretched out and felt her bones click back into place, and thought about how she should face the world. Face the hole.

And then, once she was dressed, she'd see how Stacey was.

She was sure she was fine.

Everything was fine.

Before the hole.

They just needed to sleep whatever it was off. It was just the sort of panic that comes from being in an enclosed space for too long. Being away from society for too long. Like when divers get the bends. A silly sort of panic.

They were fine.

Everything was fine.

Before the hole...

In fact, no doubt, they'd all laugh about this. Hannah felt like laughing now, the mood she was in. It was all absolutely absurd, after all. All of this, over a stupid little hole in the ground.

It was fine.

Everything... Everything was fine.

Despite the hole.

Hannah grabbed the curtains, smiled, and thought about how much she couldn't wait to see the boys. How she would hold them close, and remember the love she had for them. That her and Greg had for them. They were the light in her life, the people who brought her serenity now. They were the beautiful memories waiting to be crafted.

Hannah threw back the curtains.

And felt the air leave her lungs.

The streak of blood stretched from Rich's house to the hole.

HP Properties had moved fast.

Before any calls were placed to the police, and even before anyone could fully comprehend the grotesque scene in the centre of Anton Court, representatives had moved in and began work on controlling the situation.

Hannah stormed out of her home in a faint daze. William was also there, looking slightly more awake but no less shocked. Next to the hole a black bin bag slumped over the edge, its contents not immediately obvious, but the bloodstains that leaked from it didn't make it too tricky to guess.

By now, a raging argument was escalating between Crendon and Norris, the HP Properties man from before. As Norris tried to establish calm, Crendon only unleashed chaos, roaring a tirade that had built inside of him for a very long time.

"They're dead! They're fucking dead, Norris..."

"Yes, I am aware, Vincent, but..."

"But fucking what? We need the police here! We need... *someone* here."

"I'm here, and I'm making sure..."

"You? *You*? Who the fuck are *you*?"

"Vincent, careful..."

While Crendon continued to cry foul about the bloodbath that now accompanied the hole, it was The Colonel's turn to burst forth from his abode. While his gait was fierce and his face cemented in perpetual rage, he did not raise his voice nor do anything that would suggest impending violence. Instead, he stood by while Crendon finished his vitriol.

Hannah tried her mobile, only to find she had no signal.

"What's going on?" The Colonel said, making sure to look over at the bloody scene.

"Everything is under control," Norris said, smiling in spite of it all. "There seems to…"

"Rich went mental," Crendon said. "Murdered Stacey, and probably that Quinn fella."

Anton Court fell quiet.

"How do you know that?" William said.

Crendon gestured incredulous at the bloody bin bag. "That's not the leftovers of last night's roast now, is it?"

Hysteria was the main item on the morning's menu, but Hannah was now less pre-occupied by the murder scene that was causing the chaos, and more concerned about her lack of phone signal.

"Is your phone working?" she asked William.

He shook his head. Hannah seemed to think he already knew something.

"Crendon, can I use your phone?"

Crendon laughed, eyes wide and grin bitter. He looked over at Norris and pretended to lunge at him to incite a reaction.

"Want to tell them?"

Norris seemed to lose himself for a moment, before collecting his thoughts and resuming a state of calm.

"Mr Danforth will be along later…"

"*Later isn't now, you cunt,*" Crendon said.

Norris just glared in response.

"All I can say is, due to recent events, there will be a quarantine enforced for your own safety."

At the sound of this, the residents of Anton Court didn't fight, or cry foul. They just stood there, in silence, taking in the fresh new anarchy that the hole had brought them today.

While all was still, something fell out of the bloody bin bag.

Hannah saw it, and thought it was an arm.

She promptly vomited over the Court's road.

The morning coffee didn't quite take away the taste of sick from Hannah's mouth, but the whisky mixed into it helped.

She now found herself in her living room, staring into space and trying to piece together the shattered picture she had seen in her mind. Things like sense and logic were long deceased, taken over by a wild maelstrom of horror that never seemed to end.

One that revolved around the hole outside.

It had been William who had taken her back into her home, and supplied her with a potent beverage. Despite how hot it was, Hannah drank quickly, her senses dulled to anything like boiling beverages.

What had happened in the home of Rich Davis was recollected to her by William, who had himself been filled in by Crendon. It seemed that during the night, Rich had snapped and killed both Stacey and Quinn in their sleep. Well, Stacey was asleep at least; the bloodstains present on her bed and pillows confirmed that. Quinn's fateful location was less sure, but what was sure was that neither of them left the house in one piece.

Why Rich had decided to cut up their bodies would be lost to time, although William theorised it was to make it easier to throw them down the hole. And the reason behind that could be found in the margins of Rich's suicide note, a repeated mantra to FEED THE HOLE.

These conclusions were backed up by the presence of the bin bag by the hole. While most of the contents had ended up down the void, those that dared inspect still found various viscera present, some still in their clothes.

As for the suspect himself, the main theory was that while pouring the parts down the hole, Rich simply lost his balance and fell in. After all, he was nowhere to be found within Anton Court, and the presence of HP Properties' heavies – allegedly on call 24/7 – meant that escape was improbable.

All in all, it made for a macabre, and brutally tragic, tale.

One that Hannah couldn't quite come to terms with.

It was muscle memory that made her pick up her phone, and attempt once again to call out. She was met with the shrill beep of no reception, and in a doped loop simply ended the call and tried again.

William reached over and gently took the phone away from her.

"Line's are down," he said. "They must have some form of signal jammer active."

He didn't explain how he came to this conclusion, but William seemed to be in tune with everything that was now happening. Unlike Hannah, he was calm and collected, addressing each new absurd obstacle with complete stoicism. Despite the general chaos, he was able to pluck the relevant parts out of the mess and make sense of them, almost as if he was at home in it.

"Why would they jam our phones?" Hannah said.

"Same reason they now have guards at the gate and why the police aren't involved."

William didn't say anymore, instead offering weak reassurance in the form of a smile.

Hannah didn't want a smile. She didn't even want a Celtic Coffee. What she wanted was to speak to her boys. She wanted her freedom. And most of all, she wanted to get the hell away from the hole.

Especially when William told her what Crendon had found in Rich's home.

Among the carnage and blood, was the aforementioned suicide note. Amongst the mad scrawls and scratches was a simple message, neatly written in block capitals:

IT'S DOWN THERE

IT'S COMING UP HERE

WE'RE FUCKED

It was alarming to Hannah how quickly they all grew accustomed to their imprisonment. Much like William, both The Colonel and his wife, Heather, had foregone outrage in place of silent contemplation. They too had retired to their home, closed the door, and remained an enigma until the murder scene had been cleaned and the new order established.

While Quinn's truck remained parked near the hole, its giant reel of cable resting coiled yet limp on its bed, it no longer stood alone in blocking the entrance to Anton Court. Outside the now locked gates were two dark vehicles, carefully positioned to prevent any movement in or out of the gated community. Standing alongside them, looking like something out of a movie, were large suited individuals. They reminded Hannah of those failed bodybuilders who become guards for the rich and morally nebulous, which actually tallied with the reputation of HP Properties.

Their benevolent landlords, owners of Anton Court and countless other community builds across the country, had made sure their presence was as limited as required. Norris left as quickly as he had arrived in the morning, only giving assurances that his colleague, Danforth, would be along soon enough for an update.

This left only one real representative inside Anton Court, and he wasn't looking to help them.

Crendon was a man possessed. His face twisted bitter and ugly as he went about the walls, looking for ways to break through and allow them all to escape. It was fruitless, and the tools he carried were weak and ineffective, but he would not be stopped. He had finally had enough of the cruel whims of his employers, and was now determined to do something about it.

It wasn't just his actions, but his words, that attempted rebellion. Now the circumstances of Rich's murder-suicide were out there, Crendon was more than happy to reveal even more about the intentions of HP. The hole was deemed more important than the safety of the residents, especially the ones who had decided to stay. While legally he couldn't be told to ignore their concerns, he was not incentivised to listen to them. In fact, everything HP had told Crendon was dripping in doublespeak and interpretation.

No wonder he was mad.

Unfortunately, this only added weight to HP Properties' claim that the quarantine was due to a "shared madness" that was suspected in the aftermath of Rich's actions. HP wanted to make sure everyone who was still in Anton Court was of sound mind before leaving, lest they commit similar massacres caused by a poisoned mind.

And Crendon made sure to point toward what he believed caused this madness.

Hannah listened to his rants with a sense of fear. Long gone was the acerbic friend she grew close to after Greg's death, and instead was an angry, monstrous figure raging at an inanimate hole in the ground. He shouted curses at it, circling and spitting at it between gritted teeth. But alongside these outbursts was a damned knowledge. Much like his desire to break out of Anton Court, Crendon knew that he was powerless. It was hopeless feeling or doing anything against the hole, as that was simply what it was – a hole. It didn't matter how much value HP gave it, nor whether it did or did not have any supernatural powers, it was just a hole.

Then again, Rich's last words were now stamped on the minds of all those present. He had seen something, far down in the bowels of the earth itself. And whatever that was, it was terrifying enough to send him far beyond the void of the hole, and into an insanity that ultimately doomed him.

Right now, Hannah wondered if that same madness, that same obsession, would cause Crendon to be swallowed by the hole.

In the end, she was left just as helpless as he was.

The darkness hit with a snap.

Hannah didn't know how or when she had fallen asleep, but she knew that right now she was sitting in her living room, shrouded in the encroaching dusk. She shook as disorientation threw her about and played with her senses, making sure everything she experienced was as frightening as possible.

Eventually, the world settled down around her, and Hannah relaxed back in her chair. She closed her eyes, and let out a slow breath.

"Hello, Miss Suggs."

The voice didn't scare her as much as Hannah thought it should have. Instead, she slowly opened her eyes and looked over to the sofa on her left. Sitting there, calm and still with his hands neatly resting on his knees, was a man in a suit.

A uniform that Hannah recognised as belonging to HP Properties.

"How did you get in here?"

"We own these properties, Miss Suggs. All doors in Anton Court are open to us."

Hannah didn't like the droning tone of the suit, but didn't dare break the stillness in the air.

"Are you Danforth?"

The man shook his head.

"My name's Randolph," he said. "Danforth is far too busy to meet and greet."

"So what are you, his boss?"

Randolph didn't answer. He didn't respond at all, in fact.

"Why are you here?" Hannah said.

"A lot has happened here in Anton Court, Miss Suggs," Randolph said. "We need to make sure that you are of sound mind."

If she was honest with herself, Hannah wasn't of sound mind. But she refused to let anyone from HP Properties know that.

"I'm fine."

Randolph took this in with a hint of disbelief, a tilt of his head the only movement he had made since Hannah had recognised his presence.

"Are you sure?"

"Absolutely."

"No... obsessions?"

"Not that I know of."

"Perhaps any to do with your home?"

Hannah could see where this was going.

"Do you think I'm going to murder someone?"

The HP Properties rep didn't answer.

"I don't appreciate being kept prisoner in my home. Nor do I appreciate people just walking in like they own the place."

"We *do* own the place…"

"But we bought it from you…"

"*We*, Miss Suggs?"

Hannah winced at the implication.

"Don't you bring Greg into this."

"Greg is an integral part of this," Randolph said. "Why, he was the reason you have this property. His financial and employment situation fit well within our requirements."

"Your point being?"

"My point being you don't belong here, Miss Suggs."

"Then let me go."

Randolph slowly shook his head.

"We gave you the chance to do that," he said.

"*Then what do you want from me?*"

Randolph didn't answer. Instead, he took a slow intake of breath, and then silently kept still.

"It is our responsibility at HP Properties to assure you of your situation here in Anton Court," he said. "And that situation is thus: you are expendable. Much like Mr Davis was."

Hannah kept her cool in spite of this statement.

"Now we have an idea of the agents in play within this community, we can adjust accordingly. But you are an outlier, Miss Suggs. A proverbial fly in the ointment, if you will."

"I don't understand what you're saying."

"What I'm saying is that you are no longer under our care. You are no longer under our protection. Whatever happens to you from this moment forth is of your own fault. You will be responsible for your family losing a daughter, your children becoming orphans."

The mention of her kids made Hannah grit her teeth and growl air through her nose. She glared at Randolph and spat back her reply with venom.

"Protection from what?"

Randolph smiled. It didn't suit him.

"The hole, of course. And what it brings."

"And what's that?"

Randolph continued to smile, despite there being nowhere for his lips to stretch to.

"Something amazing, Miss Suggs. Something that will change the world."

And just like that, the dusk faded into night, and Randolph, the representative from HP Properties, faded with it.

After her impromptu visitor, Hannah made sure to put as many lights on as possible, and to flood any shadows into oblivion as she could. The idea that HP Properties and their "representatives" could easily slither into her home left her with a bad taste in her mouth, and despite being a prisoner inside Anton Court, she felt more exposed than ever.

As she threw her curtains closed, her attention was grabbed by the sight of Crendon conducting his latest rebellion against his masters. His words were lost in a storm of spat words and guttural roars, but his rage was unmistakable. It had now got the attention of those he served, with two, possibly three, guards having made their way inside the court, along with a man Hannah didn't know, but recognised as one of the aforementioned "representatives".

It was clear as well what the subject of his vitriol was. With each wild gesticulation and tense muscle spasm, Crendon kept coming back to the hole. The way he pointed and grew agitated by it was peculiar, and yet also completely sane to Hannah. The average layman would look at this scene and see a man arguing not just with a group of people calmly watching on, but a hole in the ground. Each mangled accusation, each horrified curse, was directed not at those who shared his employment with HP Properties, but the hole. Crendon seemed to loathe it just as much as they all did, but only now was he unleashing his coiled fury in the face of his bosses.

That wasn't the only movement Hannah saw. From the remaining homes that were occupied, other representatives, which she recognised as Norris and the rarely seen Danforth, made their leave and, no doubt, had cast their own warnings and threats to the Stanleys and William. Sure enough, even from across the Court and past Crendon's violent performance, Hannah could see the cold, grave eyes of The Colonel skewed in anger.

A silent plot was made between the three houses. After the invasion they had all suffered from the representatives, no one really wanted to be alone. Especially with Crendon's last stand escalating with thrown tools and pulled punches. Catching Heather's eye, Hannah made the decision to go visit her.

Especially as she saw The Colonel make his way toward William's home.

Throwing on a coat and grabbing what possessions she could think of, Hannah left what was once her sanctuary and felt the cold air of the growing dark consume her as she left. Crendon's cries were no longer silenced by double-glazing, and instead every expletive, every rant and ramble echoed through the walls of Anton Court. Still, as Hannah walked over to the Stanley residence, she couldn't make out the details of what Crendon was saying, lost to madness that had long since swallowed him whole.

One that Hannah had no doubt came from a certain pit they all danced around.

For a moment, their eyes met, and Crendon's burst of unbridled fury ceased. Hannah looked at him sadly, almost with pity. Vincent Crendon had always been the firm hand in which one could hold onto in uncertain times. He was the constant in Anton Court, the handyman who could fix anything, both material and personal. To now see him broken into a fractured disturbance of vengeance was to see a man who had finally taken too much weight and finally collapsed.

The air remained still for a moment, until Hannah looked away and kept her pace toward the Stanley residence. There, Heather also regarded Crendon with sadness. Without Hannah's eyes to distract him from the nightmare of it all, his diatribe continued to grow in volume and violence.

Hannah hoped he would be OK.

But somehow, she knew he wouldn't be.

The hole had him now.

There was something calming about entering the home of an elderly couple, especially a home that belonged to a former soldier. Hannah had no doubt that there were one or two weapons hidden among the antique dressers and cotton hangings.

Maybe that was what made her feel better being there instead of alone in her own home.

As the rambling riot of Crendon's rebellion cooled outside, Heather made sure to make Hannah feel comfortable. Tea was brewed, a plate of biscuits was offered, and a general sense of cosiness was established.

On the surface, at least. Under the skin, every nerve was tight and buzzing.

"Did you have a visitor as well?" Heather said.

"Yep. Real nice piece of shit."

Heather smiled at the profanity.

"Do you even remember falling asleep?"

Heather had asked this just before Hannah had taken a sip of her drink. The old lady chuckled.

"Don't worry, I haven't poisoned it. Neither I nor James have succumbed to the same madness as poor Richard did."

"Then why…"

"Oh James believes they gassed us," Heather said, as if this was perfectly normal. "Make it easier for them to infiltrate our homes."

Hannah began to wonder if Heather really was sane.

Then again, maybe the old woman thought the same of her.

"Did they ask about obsessions?"

Hannah nodded.

"And?"

"I suppose I have been slightly fixated…"

"On the hole, yes? I think we all have, in our own way. James certainly is, as is William Barrett. I would muster his husband Charles is equally as curious about the thing as well. Such is the way of their work."

This confused Hannah. "Their work?"

Heather sat down and sighed. She seemed to be reflecting on something, churning the cogs in order to produce a solution that would satisfy. As the silence sat heavy around them, and the soft light of the living room lamps hummed quietly, Hannah saw Heather's eyes dart around with indecision.

Ultimately, when that decision was made, it was done so with great reluctance.

"You really shouldn't be here, you know."

"Funny, they said the same thing."

"Well, sadly it's true. As a civilian you should be all tucked up in that nice hotel, alongside your boys."

Hannah gripped the cup in her hand a little harder.

"I'm sorry," Heather said, noting Hannah's disdain. "What I mean is, you should be safe away from all this. From that… hole."

"And yet, here I am, apparently ruining everybody's perfect plan."

Heather laughed.

"Listen, Heather…"

"Did I tell you how me and James met?"

Hannah left her comments linger, and sat back to listen.

"We worked together, albeit in different departments. As you know, James is a military man. And he was quite a good one, let me tell you. Many medals adorned his lapel over the years. But, he was not the man I loved. That was Clive. You remember Clive?"

"The man who crawled out the hole?"

Heather smiled. Hannah sensed a bit of venom in the old lady.

"A lovely lie that the damned thing liked to cast within me. But yes, that was Clive. He was actually one of James' fellow soldiers. I suppose these days you'd call them 'Special Forces' but, back then, they were just simply Soldiers."

"Were you a soldier?"

"I was a medic," Heather said, smiling softly at the memory. "That's how I met Clive. And James."

The room fell still as this memory floated amongst the two women, one waiting for it to be painted, the other trying to recall the shapes and colours involved. When it came to memories like the one Heather Stanley had about her husband James and her true love Clive, the picture was far too complex in parts to form properly.

In the end, all there was were the facts.

"There was an incident, as there always was in our work, and both Clive and James ended up in my ward. Clive died, as you know, and James was there."

Heather looked at Hannah with a heavy smile.

"It hasn't been a marriage of love, my dear, but it has been one of shared experience. Of companionship."

Hannah could feel herself shake. The idea of losing the one you love, so suddenly and so cruelly, hit very close to home.

"In that instance, I know how you feel," Heather said. "But I have the gift of knowledge; or maybe it's a curse. Either way, it started a path that has led us all here. To Anton Court, to watch a hole appear and ruin our lives."

"Heather?"

The old lady smiled and caught Hannah's look.

"How did you know Greg?"

Again, the fog of indecision clouded Heather's vision, but her answer wasn't mulled over for as long this time.

"The same way James and I know the Barretts. And the same way we know HP Properties and their intentions. And if you want to know more, Hannah, I could tell you. But I fear that it would be too heavy a weight for you to carry."

"Isn't that my decision to make?"

Heather laughed and shook her head.

"No. No it isn't. Your safety is what matters now."

"And what if I don't just want to sit back."

"Hannah," Heather said, "Sometimes you don't have a choice. Trust me."

The two women sat in silence and finished their tea, the slight itch of curiosity irritating the atmosphere around them.

Despite the fact her home was literally across the courtyard, Hannah happily accepted the sanctuary of the Stanleys spare room. Much like any spare room an elderly couple would have, it doubled as a storage facility full of boxed mementos and forgotten documents. Given all that had been said and inferred of late, Hannah was tempted to rifle through and see if she could learn anymore about the mysterious past of Heather and James Stanley, but a mix of morality and exhaustion meant that she simply lay on the single bed and stared at the ceiling in the gloom.

Hannah hated being on the outside of things. It was probably the only fracture that existed in her relationship with Greg. She craved knowledge and hated surprises, needing to know all the details of every little thing in order to quell any negative feelings that may stir. In her younger years, she had seen a counsellor who put it down to her need to control things, everything from the physical to the mental. If Hannah had a sense of what was going on, she could adjust it in her head to a place of comfortable understanding.

Maybe that's what attracted her to Greg. He maintained his sense of mystery, but never in a shady way. In fact, her interactions with the likes of Randolph and Heather Stanley reminded her of the way Greg would speak about his work. It was more like Heather's method than the HP rep, at once both assuring and casual. If there were any grand secrets he was keeping from her, Greg defused them to such an irrelevant level that any need to know was quashed before it grew.

Of course, with the hole now exuding its own form of control over those inside Anton Court, the questions were now too big to easily conceal. And while the answers to those questions weren't fully known, there was enough information in the minds of the Stanleys, the Barretts, and HP Properties that could assist Hannah in crafting that soothing narrative.

As it was, no answers were given, and the comforting touch had now been a firm push, now under the context of safety rather than irrelevance.

While she resisted the urge to search the spare room, Hannah's senses were hooked by the sound of the front door opening. She crept close to the room, and listened in as The Colonel returned home.

"Cup of tea?" Heather said.

The Colonel just grunted. It seemed he wasn't that different behind closed doors than he was outside of them.

"Hannah Suggs is staying with us."

There was a pause, before The Colonel replied.

"Probably best."

"She was interrogated."

"I'm not surprised."

"And threatened."

Another pause, as Hannah shut her eyes to help her hearing.

"That seems pointless, given her situation."

"Why don't they just let her go, James?"

"Because they have an asset they can potentially use," The Colonel said, the words said as dully as describing the weather.

Hannah didn't think them so innocent though. She didn't like the idea of being an asset, especially one used by HP Properties.

"Do you think…?"

"Tomorrow, breakfast," The Colonel said, and with that the voices of the Stanleys faded into another room.

More unravelled threads now rested in Hannah's mind, and it was driving her insane. Then again, she thought of what both Randolph and Heather had said about obsession, about not being able to control certain mental demands of late.

Looking out the window, Hannah saw the hole resting there silent as ever, eating the light of the moon that shone through a cloudless sky. The HP guards were gone, as were the representatives.

As was Crendon.

A realisation that made Hannah feel sick.

Day 9

It had been literal years since Hannah had woken up to the smell of freshly brewed coffee. The way the bitter, smoky aroma tickled her senses slowly awake was such a confusingly pleasant experience that, for a moment, Hannah doubted she was awake.

But awake she was, and once again she had been the recipient of a good night's sleep. No nightmares had tormented her; no visions had toyed with her inner demons. Instead, she had rested, and now felt far more alive than she had been in far too long.

Of course, this moment of serenity was just that – a moment.

Soon enough the reality came flooding back, and no matter how nice the smell of coffee was, how rested she felt, it all carried the weight of something pending; a calm before the storm, which would destroy all in its path.

Before she went and joined the Stanleys for breakfast, Hannah took another look outside at the hole. The various goons from HP Properties stood guard at the gate, preventing the interest of a couple of early onlookers. Within Anton Court itself, more intimidating figures walked around listlessly, awaiting orders as to what to do next.

Looking closer, Hannah thought they were armed.

When she arrived in the Stanleys' dining room, Heather greeted her with a smile. A healthy breakfast buffet was laid out on the table, and Hannah was reminded of the excessive enthusiasm that her own mother gave when she had visited with the boys. Maybe the lack of children in their lives had meant that, now she had the opportunity, Heather could finally unleash all those grandmother instincts that had long been dormant.

In the other room, Hannah saw that The Colonel was preparing something in a dark green holdall. Whatever it was, it clicked in a way that made her uncomfortable.

"Sleep well?"

"Too well," Hannah said, taking a seat at the table.

Heather joined her, pouring a piping hot mug of coffee for her visitor.

"There's no such thing as sleeping too well, Hannah."

"I don't know. These days a good night's sleep feels like a trap."

Heather deflected this with a chuckle. In fact, there was no talk of the hole or its effects on the residents. This meant there was barely any talk at all, especially when The Colonel joined them.

Even the way he buttered his toast and cracked open his egg was intense. Everything The Colonel seemed to do was both regimented and ferocious, a sure sign of a man who had been indoctrinated into a very specific set of rules. He didn't smile, nor make any eye contact with either Hannah or his wife. The Colonel just ate, for that was what breakfast was for.

Hannah doubted that he even saw it as food, just fuel required for the day ahead.

In fact, if it weren't for the tense knowledge of the hole outside and its strange protectors, the whole scene would seem rather normal to an outsider. The Stanleys remained dressed in knitted robes and loungewear, and the very best china was being used to serve all sorts of culinary delights.

Then it hit Hannah. This was their version of The Last Supper.

"The last breakfast," she said to herself.

That comment seemed to catch The Colonel's attention.

"You'll stay here, Miss Suggs," he said. It was less a question than an order, and Hannah didn't really appreciate it.

"Why? What are you planning, Colonel?"

Both The Colonel and Heather exchanged a look, and he swallowed a mouthful of wholemeal toast. With a stern pause, he internally debated how to respond.

Thankfully, he didn't have to, as a knock at the door saved him.

While Hannah was scared it was someone from HP, The Stanleys were far more relaxed. Opening the door revealed William Barrett, armed with several notepads and a barely functioning tablet PC. When he saw Hannah, he smiled and nodded.

"So our team is all together here, are they?"

"We're not a team," The Colonel said.

"Oh, where's your sense of adventure, James? We're on a mission now, why not enjoy it?"

The Colonel glared at William. "I don't enjoy missions. I'm not an office drone, like you."

Before any further arguments could ensue, Heather offered William a cup of coffee. He took up the offer, and took a seat at the table with Hannah. Meanwhile, The Colonel went back to the other room to continue packing.

There was an uncomfortable silence before Hannah decided to poke the bear.

"So are you going to tell me anything?"

"Has Heather told you anything?"

"Barely. She just spoke in circles."

William nodded with a big grin on his face, "that's experience for you."

"Something you share?"

"Depends on what you want to know, Hannah," William said. "I'm sure if Charles was here he'd be far more open than I would be, but then that is his way. Not one for secrets and lies is Charlie. It's one of the things I love about him."

"So what? We're just going to sit here, enjoy breakfast, and ignore the mercenaries guarding that fucking hole outside, are we?"

Heather gave William his coffee, and sat back down. He took a big gulp, wincing at the heat, before regarding Hannah with a knowing look.

"That's exactly what we're going to do. For now."

And with that, William grabbed a slice of toast and tucked in.

Everything was changing in Anton Court.

Quinn's truck, complete with his mega-reel, had gone, a black barrier had been put up to prevent folk from looking through the gate, and all the furniture from Crendon's cottage was being removed.

All under the orders of the new caretaker, a far-too cheerful guy who now wore a lost man's overalls.

Hannah watched this all happen, her attention around from the activity behind her. With William supervising, The Colonel was arranging the last of his pack, ready for a mission nobody would tell Hannah about. The only time they paid her any attention was when she announced the cable reel was gone, prompting The Colonel to emit a low growl.

"Would have been handy," he said.

"I'm sure they'll deliver you something better," Heather said, fussing around the house.

"I don't think the postman can get past that barrier," Hannah said.

"Oh, we can arrange a special delivery."

Hannah didn't bother asking any further. She didn't bother asking anything. Not what The Colonel was packing, not what William was showing him on his tablet, and definitely not whether Heather wanted any help doing whatever she was doing.

The general feeling of helplessness made Hannah antsy. The world was moving around her and she was made to just stand there, waiting for something she wouldn't be told. The whole thing made her grind her teeth and tap her foot, until she couldn't take anymore.

Without a word to the others, she went outside. She heard them call after her, but didn't bother listening.

She'd had enough.

"Who are you?" she said to the man directing the removal of Crendon's stuff.

He smiled at her, and gave a friendly salute that just made his whole shtick seem horribly overdone. He didn't give Hannah a name, instead announcing himself as the "new caretaker", and that he'd be available to help her in any way once he had finished gutting the cottage.

"Where's Crendon?"

The new caretaker's smile wavered.

"Administrative leave."

"What does that mean?"

The Caretaker looked to his right, and Hannah followed his gaze to see one of the HP guards reach for something. A shake of the head from The Caretaker, and the guard relaxed.

"I'll be sure to explain everything to you once I'm finished here, Miss…"

Hannah shook her head and laughed. This new goon didn't even know her name.

"What about the hole?" she said.

As innocuous as it had always been, the hole sat quietly in the middle of Anton Court. Hannah felt it had definitely grown in size, given that what remaining grass around it had now crumbled down its deep chasm.

Along with the bodies of Rich, Stacey, and Quinn.

"Like I say, everything will be explained…"

"Explain now."

"Hannah?"

Turning round, Hannah saw William emerge from the Stanley's home, with the elder couple slowly exiting behind him. The Colonel was carrying his large green pack, and was dressed in gear that could be best described as light fatigues.

"They've taken Crendon," Hannah said, surprising herself with the emotion in her tone.

The Caretaker just shrugged behind her, as William managed to take Hannah away from what was becoming a hot scene. She hadn't been aware, but it wasn't just that one HP guard who was reaching for a firearm.

Several of them were showing their wares, and some of their trigger fingers looked itchy.

"This isn't your fight," William said.

"Yes it is! They want to take it all away from us, William, and for what? A fucking hole?"

"It's not just the hole…"

"Oh, of course it isn't. It's more than a hole, but you can't tell me, right?"

William sighed.

"They probably dug the damn thing themselves in order to do… whatever it is they're doing."

"They didn't dig it, Hannah."

"If they did, they're murderers. They're responsible for Rich killing Stacey."

"Hannah, they didn't dig the hole. No one did."

Hannah stopped ranting for a moment, trying to work out what William was saying.

For once, he decided to give her a nugget of information.

"The hole wasn't created up here. It was created…"

Instead of finishing this sentence, William just pointed down.

As Hannah tried to digest this, and The Caretaker took note of The Colonel making his way over, none of them noticed the trio of figures walking out of the Cooper residence.

It was Hannah who first caught a glimpse of the new visitors to Anton Court, although it only served to further her confusion.

"Perry?"

Sure enough, one of the three people to emerge from the Coopers' home was Perry, the liaison that Hannah had been assigned to help deal with Greg's death. Dressed in a casual suit, she smiled at Hannah with an enthusiastic wave, and made a beeline toward her to grasp her in an embrace.

"Hannah, how are you?" Perry said.

Hannah stood there, utterly confused before managing a response. "I've been better."

"I can imagine. There's a lot going on, and I'm sure you have lots of questions. For now, though, I need to deal with these gents here and then we can catch up and talk about how you're doing."

The gents Perry referred to were the HP guards, who were none too happy to see new people suddenly appear in Anton Court. The Powers That Be had informed them that no one was to enter or leave the gated community, so having Perry and company arrive was met with armed threats and stern looks.

This escalation made Hannah nervous, but she was amazed to see how calmly Perry and her partner – introduced as Stewart – dealt with the situation. The guards barked questions toward them, demanding how they got here and what they were doing.

Perry's answer was simple:

"The door was open, and we're here about *that*."

That, being the hole.

William tried to placate Hannah, but she wasn't willing to remove herself as a spectator to this spectacle. While HP's goons were loud and aggressive, Perry and Stewart remained joyfully stoic, standing alongside The Colonel and Heather as they waited to do... something.

In her head, some threads of an idea were snatching at each other to tell Hannah what that something was.

All that was fried as she took note of the third member of Perry's group. At first glance, they didn't seem there, resembling the kind of figure who caught the corner of your eye. But when Hannah managed to focus on them, she felt a severe pain crash inside her head, and a wave of nausea overwhelm her.

The person looked out of place. Their general shape was obscured by a visual blur that made it difficult to even see if they were a man or a woman. At times, Hannah thought she could see them clearly, but she'd blink and they'd sharply shift out of focus again. She tried to ask William who they were, but found the words lacking and her head swelling with pain. Instead, Hannah found herself being escorted toward the Cooper household, dizzy from the prolonged exposure to this stranger.

What unnerved her most was that this person did not engage, and did not seem to be interested in joining Perry and Stewart's calming of the conflict with HP. Instead, they watched, and made sure to note Hannah as she skimmed past them.

While also noting what was going on between the rival groups.

And the hole.

With grey eyes that made Hannah feel even more sick.

Being one of the only two families on Anton Court with children, Hannah had visited the Cooper house many times over the months. As she entered it now, she was reminded of all the times she would go over with the boys, and let them play with the Coopers' daughter while engaging in more parental conversations than the ones she had with Charles. Tim and Louise's family pictures still adorned the walls and shelves, and Samantha's toys remained strewn in various rooms. The only things missing, of course, were the Coopers themselves.

Not that this mattered anymore, as this was no longer *their* home. It was a base of operations for whatever authority Perry was part of, and she had already, along with her colleagues Stewart and the grey figure, made what was a dining room into something more official.

In addition to arranging several computers upon a table, and placing unusual equipment about the place, Perry and company made sure to engage heavily with William and the Stanleys, The Colonel in particular. Settling into a familiar soft chair, Hannah looked on in a daze as the group looked serious and spoke in firm, technical language.

As she watched on, William placed his tablet onto the table, prodded at the screen, and somehow projected an image into the air. It looked like a long, tapered funnel, which Hannah immediately recognised despite its unusual dimensions.

It was the hole.

The struggle to comprehend all this was beginning to thump inside Hannah's skull. The presence of the grey person didn't help; although the nausea had eased since she made the choice to not look directly at them, now combined with the intense and confusing activity happening around her, she felt like the world was underwater.

"Tea?"

Almost like she was snapping out of trance, Hannah looked to see Perry standing before her, mug in hand.

"A cup of tea always solves everything, I find. Typical British way, isn't it?"

"What... what's going on?" Hannah said.

"Listen, you... mistakes were made. And I'm slightly guilty of that. Trust me, August has let me know."

Perry referred to the grey person, who seemed to be both simultaneously watching their conversation and the discussion happening over the image of the hole.

"Is that what I think it is?"

"Yes. William did a survey on it and thinks he has a... you know what? I'm getting ahead of myself. You don't need to know this."

Once again, Hannah was finding the doors to information slowly closing in front of her.

"No, I'd like to know," she said.

"I think what's best is that we get you with the boys, Jarelle and Warren, eh?"

"No, I want to know what's going on."

"It's just a lot of silly government stuff happening that you really..."

"Government stuff?"

"Again, it's nothing really…"

Hannah felt her whole body begin to convulse. Her heart beat faster than it should, her muscles went into spasm under her skin, and her nerves were firing far too fast for her brain to react.

Eventually, it became too much.

"What the *fuck* is going on?"

The discussion at the dining table stopped. Everyone's attention was directed at the hysterical woman in the soft chair, who Perry was trying, and failing, to calm down.

But as quickly as it had snatched them away from what they were talking about, they lost interest and went back to their planning.

Hannah looked up at Perry, the person who had been looking after her ever since Greg had died. She had never questioned this, never wondered who she was or what she did or whom she, or even Greg, worked for. These were all questions that seemed unimportant - part of a puzzle that was of no interest to Hannah. But since the hole appeared, and since everyone had gone crazy and HP Properties had turned into an evil corporation and people had died, Hannah wanted to know everything.

And she finally didn't want to be given vague proclamations or pithy statements.

"Perry, tell me the truth."

Perry didn't smile like she always had for Hannah. She didn't exude an aura of calming placation or understanding. Instead, she looked cold, all emotion rendered void to be replaced with a more pragmatic approach.

"Come with me," she said.

"I'm staying here," Hannah said.

"You're going to come with me."

Hannah found herself forcefully lifted and pulled toward another room of the Cooper residence, up the stairs and along the corridor, until she found herself in the ambient calm of Tim and Louise's bedroom. Pastel colours coated every inch of the room, from the wallpaper to the bedding, and as Perry deposited Hannah down upon it, dragging a chair from the corner, the mood seemed to poison the environment.

"You want to know what's going on?" Perry said.

"Perry…"

"*Agent* Perry."

Hannah looked shocked, and a little confused, at the brusque manner Perry had announced this. Noting her reaction, Perry loosened up and let out a long, heavy sigh.

"Perry's fine."

"Right. So you work for the government, *Agent* Perry?"

"Of sorts. More alongside the government."

"And who else works alongside the government here in Anton Court?"

"I think you're clever enough to know that, Hannah."

Hannah felt herself tense up before she asked her next question.

"Greg?"

Perry didn't answer. Hannah presumed this was because she didn't want to repeat herself.

"What's going on here, Perry? What's that hole all about? Why are you, and HP, so interested…?"

"I get why you want to know these things, Hannah. Everybody does. Everybody likes to know the ins and outs of what's going on in the world. Except, you don't. Not really."

Hannah didn't understand.

"People like yourself, everyday people, want their beliefs confirmed. They want their view of the world to be reinforced and anything that may go against that, well that's just something that needs to be solved to fit into that worldview."

"You'd be surprised how open-minded I am," Hannah said.

"Hannah, with all due respect, your mind could be as open as the bloody ocean, and still it wouldn't be large enough to even grasp an inkling of what is happening here."

Before Hannah could argue, Perry viciously leant forward.

"Don't believe me? Then think about how you felt seeing August?"

Even the memory of the shimmering figure made Hannah feel ill.

"There are many wheels that turn below the surface, Hannah. Many cogs and mills that spin, crunch, and work together to keep everything running. Some of these things run in ways that defy what you were taught at school. Some things are morally *against* what your parents told you was right. But without them?"

Perry snapped her fingers and sat back.

The two women sat in silence for a moment, before Hannah composed herself and looked Perry dead in the eyes.

"Is that what the hole is then? Access to this… fucked up machine?"

Perry laughed, shaking her head.

"Then what is down there, Perry?"

The words didn't immediately come, as Perry decided what the best and worst things to say were. Eventually, she decided to stick with the basics.

"Stanley is going to find out."

Hannah couldn't believe this.

"The Colonel is going down the hole?"

Perry remained silent, awaiting further indignation.

"But he's an old man, Perry!"

"And yet he's far fitter than you or I."

Perry smiled, but Hannah wasn't in the mood. She was horrified at the thought of the elderly Colonel going down that hole, not just because of what was down there that fried Rich's brain, but also because he had no means to get down there. She wondered what he would end up doing.

Jump?

"We can't have you here, Hannah," Perry said. "It's not safe."

Hannah only vaguely listened.

"Trust me. Things are going to happen that are… well, way outside what is messing with your head right now."

The boys were still safe, Hannah was sure of that. Call it a mother's sixth sense. Maybe that was one of the wheels that Perry talked about.

"We can easily get you out of here. We have… methods that can have you extracted back to the hotel with Jarelle and Warren, and…"

"I'm not leaving."

Perry's mouth hung open at this statement.

Hannah just glared at her.

"After everything I've been through? Losing Greg? Having you talk to me whenever I felt like giving up? Keeping the boys sane? Dealing with that *fucking* hole?"

"Hannah, realistically, what the Hell do you think you can *do* here?"

It was Hannah's turn to smile.

It wasn't a friendly one.

"Learn."

"Learn what?"

"Learn what's going on."

As the two women sat there in tense silence, there was a courtesy knock at the room's door. It ended up being Heather who appeared before Hannah and Perry.

"They're here," she said, before disappearing again.

Hannah couldn't help but let out a mocking snicker. "Who is it this time? Supersoldiers? Aliens from outer space?"

"No," Perry said, getting up with a sigh, "it's your landlords."

Curious, Hannah looked out the window to see a large stretch limo slowly manoeuvre itself into Anton Court. Unlike most of the heavy-duty apparel the HP guards seemed to don, this vehicle positively shone in spite of the day's gloom with its silver paint job, one that made no effort to hide the various reinforcements applied to the car.

The first people to get out were more guards, who were less discreet with their firearms. Holding their rifles carefully, and scanning Anton Court from behind dark shades, they signalled to each other before one side of the vehicle opened up.

From within, a man in a wheelchair rolled out, followed by another old man armed with a cane.

That was enough for Hannah to go investigate further.

Once she was down the stairs of the Cooper residence, Hannah saw that William, Stewart, and The Colonel were still busy looking over the projection of the hole. Heather was talking to Perry, while the blurry figure known as August was watching outside.

They were the only one to notice Hannah leaving the house.

Once outside, Hannah saw that the two elderly visitors had made their way to the hole, where the new caretaker was speaking to them. He was rather animated, making a lot of gestures and looking quite excited, something that was not shared by his audience.

As she approached, some of the guards gripped their rifles a bit tighter, but it was the caretaker who made sure Hannah wasn't shot.

"Miss Suggs, can I…"

"Who are you?" she said, ignoring the caretaker and fixing her glare at the elderly newcomers.

As they turned to face her, she saw that the man with the cane wore thick, shaded goggles that encased his eyes, while the man in the wheelchair resembled a melted version of Munch's The Scream. He seemed to have no jaw, instead the lower half of his gaunt face hanging in a constant gasp.

"Miss Hannah Suggs?" the goggled man said, offering his hand. "I'm Mr Harwood, of HP Properties. This is Mr Phelps."

Phelps didn't look as friendly as Harwood, not that Hannah had any plans to become pals with the creepy couple.

"So you're the men who own this place?" she said.

"We own Anton Court, yes."

"ALONG WITH OTHER DEVELOPMENTS," a metallic voice said from a speaker in Phelps' wheelchair.

"Good. Good. Because I want to ask some questions."

"Oh, no need for questions, Miss Suggs," Harwood said, his thin lips stretching into a sickly smile. "In fact, I'm sure you already know the answers."

"SHE'S NOT ONE OF THEM."

This seemed to surprise Harwood.

"PARTNER WAS. HE'S DEAD."

"Oh, well, then surely you should have left by now?"

"This is my home."

Harwood chuckled. "Oh no. No, no. Your house is *our* home. All of Anton Court is ours. You're merely a tenant, and your lease is no longer valid."

Hannah couldn't believe what she was hearing. She was sorely tempted to grab the old man and throw him down his precious hole. Instead, she felt someone pull her back.

She turned round to see William holding onto her, shaking his head silently as she went to protest. As he dragged her away, Hannah watched as Perry and Stewart arrived, acting calmly toward Harwood and Phelps, and mocking the fact their guards were so heavily armed.

As they got closer to the Cooper household, Hannah shook away William's grip, and turned on him.

"Why the fuck did you do that?"

"Hannah…"

"I was going to ask them about the hole. Or, actually, they already thought I *knew* about the hole, which made me fucking laugh!"

As Hannah raged at William, The Colonel appeared with Heather and August, holding a large box. She watched as the Stanleys walked toward the hole, where Perry and Stewart were still deep in debate with the elderly Harwood and Phelps, while August stopped to take in the growing confrontation.

"And you can fuck off as well!" she said, wincing at August.

William stood there shaking his head as Hannah hopped from foot to foot, itching to do something, anything. Her gaze darted between William and the group congregating around the hole, where The Colonel placed his box. This seemed to inspire more debate, and a shade more aggression from the HP guards.

"Oh, great, now they're going to bloody shoot us all," Hannah said.

"No. They never do."

The monotone reassurance came from August, who watched alongside Hannah at the developments before them. Before anyone could react, both Harwood and Phelps made their way back to their vehicle, with Harwood in particularly high spirits. Before entering the car, he paused, and looked over to where Hannah stood. With a wave, he shouted over to her.

"Everything is inevitable, Miss Suggs," he said.

As he vanished into the car, Phelps had spun his wheelchair around to glare one final time at Hannah. As they stared at each other, Hannah felt cold, feeling both angry and sick at the arrogance she had just bore witness to.

Not that she had time to think about this more, as while the vehicle drove around the central garden that the hole had consumed, The Colonel was connecting himself to his box.

Once both Harwood and Phelps were driven away, the whole entourage of guards belonging to HP Properties seemed to disappear too.

All that was left of the insidious property developers was the new caretaker – now known simply as Mick – and the recognisable smarm of HP reps Norris and a woman named Greene. However, none of them seemed bothered to engage with their counterparts, instead retiring to what used to be Crendon's cottage with wide smiles and confident gaits.

They didn't even seem to care about the activity that was now taking place by the hole. After setting up his strange box, The Colonel had begun to organise various items in his green pack, while Heather inspected the box itself. Still reeling from everything that was happening, Hannah stood there a moment wondering what she should do next.

In the end, she just sat down on the grass.

"Need a chair, my dear?"

To her surprise, Hannah looked up to see the beaming face of Charles Barrett. He placed a couple of seats in the Cooper's front garden, and offered a hand for Hannah to get back up.

"How did you…?"

"The door was open," Charles said. "Now I understand you've been a bit feisty?"

Hannah laughed. It was only mildly out of a sense of amusement. Everything that had happened in the past few hours had left her drained, speechless, and utterly confused. The fact that Anton Court had suddenly turned into ground zero for a face-off between a property company and weird agents of an unknown organisation made her head spin just thinking about it.

And now, seemingly from out of nowhere, her closest friend in the community had returned from a hotel miles away, as jovial as ever.

All because of a hole.

"Do you know what's going on?" she said.

"Probably just as much as you, Han. But then again, maybe the same quantity, just different parts."

"Charles, I've had enough of people talking in circles around me."

"Oh, well get used to it, dear girl, because that's what we're all trained in," Charles said with a wink.

Hannah immediately picked up that Charles was also a member of the mysterious group that seemingly everyone else in Anton Court was part of. She shook her head and went to leave, when Charles stopped her.

"I know what it's like, being a spectator to the unusual, but trust me when I say that this is all... normal."

Hannah scoffed. "Normal?"

"Well, standard then."

Charles waved his hands to try and say something, but nothing came. Instead, he merely shrugged.

"You know what? Part of me doesn't even care anymore," Hannah said, watching as Heather finished tinkering with the box and waited on The Colonel to finish working on something in his pack.

"That's probably best."

"Easy for you to say. You're one of *them*."

It was Charles's turn to scoff. "I'm not nearly as important as you think I am, Han. I'm just here because William is. My expertise is in the arts, and in my research there isn't much about that hole from the renaissance or cubist periods."

Hannah laughed, genuinely. It felt good to finally embrace some levity after so long vacationing in the mental gloom.

Sitting there with Charles, watching the Stanleys work away next to the hole, Hannah finally managed to relax. She closed her eyes, let the afternoon sun peck at her from between the clouds, and thought about her boys. She knew she had neglected them, all because of the damn hole, and now more than anything wished to see them again.

Maybe if Charles could come back so easily, they could too.

Before she could ask if that was possible, both she and Charles noticed things getting emotional near the hole. The Colonel had finished tinkering with his pack, had slung it over his shoulder, and begun to affix a harness around his gaunt frame. As Heather fussed over him, pulling on parts of the material to make sure it was secure, Hannah saw a brief glimpse of the elderly couple she had grown to know.

Two individuals – one meek, one angry – working together in spite of themselves, the definition of opposites attracting.

Then, as The Colonel connected his harness to a rope that he pulled from the box, the couple paused. Hannah felt the world around them remain still, completely unaware of anyone else standing alongside where she and Charles sat watching, as the Stanley's looked at each other.

With a tender hand, Heather stroked The Colonel's face and closed her eyes. The Colonel, more formally know as James Stanley, took her comforting hand and held it tight, kissing it gently. He pulled himself toward his wife, embraced her with a grasp Hannah had only seen in the most loving partners in history, and kissed her.

As the moment melted away, the Stanleys gazed into each other's eyes. James Stanley smiled. Heather Stanley smiled with him. He let go of her.

And then jumped in the hole.

Even though she knew it was going to happen, Hannah still couldn't believe that it actually had.

The Colonel, an old man in his late 60s or early 70s, had just jumped feet first down the hole that had been plaguing Anton Court for over a week; a hole that had devoured the central garden in the community, driven those living there mad, and caused the death of one household.

The last thing Hannah thought was necessary was another victim fed into the abyss.

Running over to the hole, Hannah took note of the box that The Colonel had left there. It wasn't that large, probably no bigger than your average moving box, but was lined with steel and reinforced into the ground via four pincers that gripped into the concrete. Through a slit in the front, a thin rope unspooled, whistling with speed as The Colonel abseiled down the holes walls.

Hannah didn't say anything. There was nothing really to say. No arguments or condemnations against those around her. Her world – the entire world in fact – had gone insane and she felt like the only sane person left.

After being grabbed by Heather to prevent her joining The Colonel down the hole, Hannah felt dizzy and watched the world turn to fog.

When she came to, she was back in the horribly quaint pastel bedroom of the Coopers. The combination of teal and pink made her grimace, and the sight of the constantly blurry August sitting beside her actually helped her feel more comfortable.

"You nearly fell in," they said. "Sometimes, you do."

Hannah didn't understand, instead clenching her eyes closed to appease the growing pain in her head.

"Is it safety that concerns you? As if it is, it is of little consequence."

"You sent an old man to his death."

"Possibly. In my experience that only occurs approximately 60% of the time."

The look Hannah gave August in that moment was usually saved for random weirdoes out at bars, or stubborn conspiracy theorists. Whoever August was, and whatever they did, it was very strange to say the least.

"Maybe I should just go and be with my boys," she said, rubbing her forehead.

August's stoicism perked up for a moment. "Invariably, you don't."

"Can you see the future or something?"

"Future. Past. Present. They're all the same to people like me."

"And who are people like you?"

"They call us Grounding Agents. Individuals who can exist in infinite times across infinite space."

Hannah went back to being confused.

"You see why they don't tell you everything."

"You're mad."

August nodded in agreement.

Sitting up, Hannah noticed it was getting dark out. She thought again of The Colonel diving deeper in the hole outside, and feared what he would find at the bottom.

Especially if it was the same thing Rich found.

"OK, if you are existing in… *infinite spaces*… then do you know what's down there?"

"It depends," August said.

"On what?"

"On time. And space. Amongst other variables."

Hannah huffed in frustration. She flung herself around and off the bed, and went to leave.

Before doing so, she looked back at August.

"Not going to stop me?"

"Makes no difference."

"Of course. You already know whether you do or not…"

"Sometimes I do, sometimes I don't. Such is the state of infinity."

"Then how do you stay sane?" Hannah said, her attention briefly diverted from leaving.

"Only the most mentally firm enter into my role. You have to possess the capability to believe and accept anything."

"That's a lot to take in."

August finally turned to Hannah, their grey eyes making sure to directly meet hers. Their face betrayed no emotion, nor any sort of static features, instead shimmering before Hannah.

"What if I told you a story?"

Hannah's eyes narrowed.

"About?"

"Well, by now you're used to how we speak in metaphors and analogies, so perhaps a story will help put your mind at ease. Or not."

Hannah moved back to the bed and sat down, curious as to what August was saying.

"Does it?"

"Put your mind at ease?"

"Yeah."

"Sometimes."

It was hard to tell, but in certain brief moments it looked like August was smiling.

Or was very, very sad. It was hard for Hannah to tell.

"Do you know of eggs?" August said.

"Eggs?"

"The kind that comes from chickens."

"I know what eggs are."

"Indeed. Then as you can know, the life that grows inside an egg is subject to very specific environmental requirements to live. It needs a certain amount of heat, a certain amount of light, to help with incubation."

Hannah thought this was a weird story. Then again, coming from this August person, that wasn't wholly a surprise.

"An egg is oval shaped. It is blessed with a firm, outer husk in which to protect the being inside, until it is ready to hatch. But that can only occur, as I say, under the right circumstances. The perfect environment."

"Right," Hannah said.

August gestured a sphere with their hands, gazing into the centre as they paused.

"Consider, Hannah Suggs, what else has benefitted from a perfect environment. An exact combination of heat and light, in order to live, to thrive."

Hannah didn't get it.

"This planet; perfectly placed to benefit from a central sun to nurture life. To help beings grow. To incubate them until they can hatch."

August finished their story, and got up from their chair. As they left, Hannah sat there thinking over what they had just said, and what it meant.

She was beginning to see why everyone had spoken to her the way they did. The alternative was…

Well, the alternative made her head hurt even more.

Downstairs, things had started to pick up.

While William and Charles spoke over diagrams on their shared tablet, Perry and August discussed something in hushed tones. Over at what used to be the Cooper's dining table, Heather and Stewart sat next to a laptop, waiting.

As Hannah arrived, they didn't have to wait much longer.

"Is this bloody thing working?"

The voice over the laptop's speaker belonged to The Colonel. He had been fitted with a fancy headset, and was making sure he had contact with those above ground.

The moment of relief from Heather quickly melted away as the serious business of the hole took precedence.

"How far down are you, James?" Stewart said.

"Far enough," The Colonel said, his tone showing no immediate difference than it would if he were complaining about his garden. "Maintaining enough descending speed not to splatter myself against the walls, but not so slow as it'll take me bloody days to get down there."

For some reason, it was grounding to Hannah to hear The Colonel speak in such a manner. Despite all the madness around her, all the strange events and unusual figures arriving, there was a constant normality in the grumpy old man who lived across from her.

With the others now concentrating on what The Colonel was saying, he explained the monotony of his descent so far; there had been no dangers, no strange occurrences, just the same walls that Rich had described before.

"So there are no environmental changes?" Charles said.

"Is that Barrett?"

"Aw, he remembers me," he said to Hannah with a smile.

"I thought he had buggered off to look into some scrolls or whatnot."

Charles smile faded.

"Anyway, to answer your question, yes, there are some environmental changes. The walls seem slicker than when that idiot Davis went down. Nothing to worry about though. Doesn't seem to be the same corrosive material that ate that chap's finger. Otherwise I'd be split open like an overcooked pie."

The Colonel did confirm that the hole was tapering, much like they had all seen in William's projection. His speedier descent meant that The Colonel noticed it more, and the further down he got, the tighter it was getting.

And that wasn't all. Much like Rich had said, the temperature of the hole wasn't what one would expect. It seemed to settle at a comfortable, ambient temperature, but The Colonel noted that he could feel a warm rush of air coming from below his position.

"It's not a wind," he said, "but it's definitely something. Very warm, and a little moist."

The group exchanged looks, which Hannah interpreted as "shit".

"How easy would it be to ascend?" Stewart asked.

The Colonel laughed. "You think I'd arm myself if I thought I was coming back?"

Hannah's concern quickly returned. She knew The Colonel liked his firearms, but the thought of him going into the hole with one – at the very least – was worrying. After all, why would he need a gun?

Part of her knew the answer, and quickly buried it away in the deepest part of her brain.

"How long until you reach the bottom?" Perry said.

Silence. Hannah looked across the room and noted August was writing something down.

"If our estimations are correct, Agent Perry, then there is no bottom."

"You know what I mean."

The Colonel laughed again, albeit a little less heartily this time around.

"Within the hour. Depending on how far I want to drop at any given time. Personally, I'd like to avoid terminal velocity…"

Most of the group moved away from the table, satisfied at what they heard. Hannah watched them as they convened in groups, made various moves to reassure the other, or in the case of August, carried on tapping on their computer.

The only person aside from Hannah who remained at the laptop was Heather. Sitting with her, she saw how proud the old lady looked. Even though she couldn't see her husband, Heather looked at the screen with a smile that was warm enough to heat the whole room.

Part of her was jealous of that look, but then Hannah knew that if Greg were there, he may well be doing the same thing The Colonel was.

Or whatever the likes of the Barretts, Perry, Stewart, and August were doing.

As she got lost in her own head, Hannah felt a hand on her shoulder.

"Would you like to help me?" Heather said.

Hannah tried to argue her growing feeling of uselessness, but Heather had already anticipated it and was ready to bat it away.

"We're just listening, that's all."

Hannah smiled, quietly thanking Heather for making her a part of the whole thing rather than try to distract her with abstract mumbo-jumbo. As she settled next to her, Heather leant in close.

"Besides, means I can get us some tea. And go to the loo."

With a chuckle, the two women sat quietly at the laptop, waiting for The Colonel to report in again.

Unlike when Rich had ventured down the hole, The Colonel didn't subject those listening to an on-going commentary. In fact, when he did speak, it was in clipped sentences that were to the point, and mostly based in fact. Heather listened and wrote down anything that seemed interesting, while Hannah made sure to respond accordingly in various affirmations and exclamations.

It was good to be part of what was going on, even if Hannah was still in the dark about most things. By now, she had tried to convince herself not to care, that it was obviously information that she didn't need to know. Besides, her cryptic conversation with the blurry August had left her with a bigger headache than normal.

The strange figure was standing with their colleagues, Perry and Stewart, at the front window of the Coopers. They were watching something closely, with August being the main recipient of the conversation. Occasionally, they would look at their device, tap away, and feed back whatever was on the screen to the two women.

As for the Barretts, they were enjoying catching up. Hannah thought it quite cute that, in spite of the work they were attempting to do, the odd moment of affection or flirtation still popped up.

It made her miss her own family.

It made her miss Greg.

"They're moving," Stewart said.

Everyone's attention turned to the window. Hannah remained with Heather at the laptop, despite the urge to insert herself in the latest situation.

"What's the engagement odds?" Perry said.

"Not enough," August said, their voice flat and emotionless.

"Good. I can't be bothered with a fire-fight at this stage."

"Darling, remember we're academics, not soldiers," Charles said.

Perry laughed, shaking her head. She wandered over to where the Barretts were sitting, and looked over at Hannah. In that moment, Perry found herself realising Hannah was still present, and what that meant.

"Hannah, are you…?"

Hannah just put her hands up to stop Perry speaking. "I'm fine."

"If you do want to leave, we can…"

"She's helping me with James," Heather said, aware that Hannah wasn't going to change her mind soon. The laptop crackled as The Colonel responded to his name, before going back to the ambient sound of his descent.

Perry sat at the table, and looked at Hannah. She was smiling, and reminded Hannah of the woman who had counselled her since Greg's passing, rather than the stern "agent" that had suddenly arrived in Anton Court.

"I would say I'm sorry you're here to witness this, but then again, I guess you were always going to."

"Is that what your friend says," Hannah said, nodding toward August.

Perry laughed. "August has told you about their work, then. Did you understand it?"

"Barely."

The women laughed, again prompting a confused response from The Colonel.

"If Greg was here, he'd be proud of you, you know?"

Hannah smiled.

"He was the one who suggested the implant here in Anton Court. He had gathered the intel regarding Harwood and Phelps and what they were planning. It was on his suggestion that we include William, Charles, and the Stanleys."

For a moment, Perry looked into the distance, the sadness of her friend's passing hitting her.

She soon regained her professional composure.

"We're supposed to be the ones who 'save the world', as silly as that sounds. I mean, if I told you some of the things we've seen…"

"Budapest?" Charles said.

"Don't remind the poor woman," William said.

Heather just laughed.

"Indeed," Perry said. "My point is, Greg wasn't just a great man, Hannah, he was one of the best. It was a cruel irony that it was a car wreck that got him."

Hannah let the silence answer for her. She gritted her teeth and held back the tears that threatened to come, and instead recalled the good times she had with Greg. The laughs they had shared, the fun they'd had with Jarelle and Warren.

All taken away because of a moment of stupidity from another human being, and the random violence of a motor vehicle.

And now, here she was, listening to an old man descend a strange hole, while two rival agencies fought around it.

Greg would have laughed himself into a stupor.

"There's that smile," Perry said.

Hannah just sighed and shrugged. "Gotta smile about something, haven't you?"

In a casual move made by many people before her, Perry idly scanned the room. It wasn't until her eyes met August's, that Hannah saw her smile fade.

The shimmering agent was looking grim, a far cry from their usual neutral expression.

Without a word, Perry got up and joined her fellow suits. Before Hannah could say anything, there was word from the laptop.

"I've found something," The Colonel said. "And it isn't pretty."

It seemed to Hannah that things had taken a turn both above and below the surface.

While Perry joined Stewart and August in some animated discussion, The Colonel confirmed he had reached what he called "the choke point" of the hole. It had been the area that Rich had noted was where the hole got uncomfortably tight, although as The Colonel reassured those listening, his thinner physique meant it would be easier to navigate.

His problem, however, was what was blocking his progress.

"I've found Davis."

The Colonel clarified that he had found the body of Rich Davis. According to his description, upon falling down the hole without the steadying application of a rope, Rich's body had plummeted at speed. With this new knowledge, The Colonel theorised that some of the fresh residue on the walls of the hole actually were the blood and assorted matter of Rich Davis, cracked open and sprayed with each collision.

Now, The Colonel explained, Rich's body had lodged itself in the holes tightening spot. Not that it was in any condition to retrieve – The

Colonel explained that his neck was broken at a right angle, and several broken bones that had torn through the skin were wedged into the walls. Within the tight confines, Rich's body resembled a bloody pretzel more than a man.

As soon as Hannah went to ask how The Colonel planned to get past this obstruction, she wished she hadn't.

"Well, I'm going to stomp the damn fool down his precious hole."

As an oxymoronic ambience of soft squelches and hard crunches echoed through the laptop speakers, Hannah distracted herself with the goings on of Perry's team. They were gathered around August's device, and not looking glad at what was on there. As always, August spoke to them without emotion and without distress, although it was clear that something was very, very wrong.

Excusing herself for a glass of water, Hannah went to the kitchen, smiling at Charles's request for one of their 'special' coffees. Instead, she turned on the tap and filled a glass, carefully drinking the contents. Doing so, Hannah was surprised to see her hand shaking. She had been doing well to put her nerves to one side and concentrate on what was happening, but now she was alone once more, the reality – whatever that meant anymore – was settling in.

Out the kitchen window, Hannah saw the people from HP setting up their camera. Norris was on his phone, smiling broadly and making all sorts of gestures. Once again, Hannah felt the bile rise up inside her. She grew angry at the invasion that had taken place here in Anton Court, in her own home. She resented Perry's presence alongside her weirdo so-called "agents", and how they had made what was supposed to be a calm place into a zone of insanity.

Most of all, she hated the hole. She hated it. The fact it was so innocuous to the average eye, and yet contained so much horror, so much filth and rot, that she couldn't wait to see it defeated in some way. Because it wasn't just something that could be filled or plastered over, Crendon and his friend Ronnie found that out the hard way. It was alive, and taunting her. It ate up not just the light that shone into it, but the ground around it and the minds of those who saw it. It gave them a taste of their own obsessions, their own insecurities, and like any other enabler made them want more until it destroyed them.

The hole in Anton Court wasn't just a hole. It was darkness, a void that was cruel and apathetic to the ways of the residents. It just wanted to consume, to devour, until there was nothing else left to eat.

"Water?"

Breaking out of her furious stupor, Hannah found in her rage she had shaken most of the glass's contents onto the floor. She relaxed the tension in her scowl and released her muscles, and turned to face the curious August.

"Takes away a percentile, but not enough," they said.

"You all look very worried."

August didn't respond, instead tilting their head in an ambivalent manner.

"Should *we* be worried?"

"Always be worried, Hannah Suggs. For there's more to this world than you can imagine."

"Yeah you said. Eggs."

August let out a brief laugh, but their face did not showcase amusement. Or maybe it did, it was hard for Hannah to tell.

"You know, you never disappointed me," August said.

Hannah looked confused. "Thank you?"

"Until now."

August retrieved what looked like a handle from their suit jacket, latched it onto a nearby cupboard door, and pressed some buttons. Before doing anything more, they turned to Hannah.

"Spend time with your children, Hannah Suggs. Don't let the hole take them from you, too."

While their words stunned Hannah, August pulled open the cupboard door to reveal a bright, sterile room behind it. They detached their handle, walked through the frame of the door, and closed it behind them.

When Hannah reopened it, she found nothing but various supplies stacked neatly on shelves.

Seeing a pack of children's novelty biscuits, she burst into tears.

The harsh truth that Hannah had casually neglected her own children in her addiction to the hole left her kneeling on the floor, retching with emotion. She wailed so hard and so loud that everyone had immediately come to her aid, distressed at her outburst.

Despite various offers of help and assistance, there was only one thing that Hannah wanted now.

"I want my boys," she sobbed.

Thankfully, this wasn't an impossible task.

Through the same methods that Perry and company had arrived, that Charles had returned, and that August had left, so did Jarelle and Warren Suggs enter the Cooper household all the way from the Garry Hotel.

The reunion was as beautiful and fraught with emotion as one would expect, and for a long time Hannah wouldn't let go of her two children. The three of them cried, laughed, and lived in a brief moment where the world wasn't falling apart around them. Once calm was restored and ruffled hairs were swept away from young foreheads, Hannah had asked them how they had got here.

Jarelle's answer wasn't a surprise.

"The door was open," he said, almost confused at the question.

It didn't matter now how they had arrived back at Anton Court, all that did was that Hannah had her two wonderful boys in her arms again. She kept them close to her, no longer intrigued by The Colonel's descent down the hole, the plots of HP outside, or the plans of everyone else present.

She had the most important people in the world with her, once more.

As the others went back to whatever it was they were doing, Hannah led Jarelle and Warren upstairs. While the two boys were eager to return to their own rooms and bed, the situation outside didn't make Hannah comfortable walking them over there. Besides, while she was now dedicated to being with her boys, she also didn't want to stray too far from the security that Perry and company provided. Therefore, there was only one option.

"A *girl's* bed?"

The boys had shared a bed before, and they would do so again for now. While the pastel monstrosity of the Cooper's main bedroom was an option, in Hannah's mind it was more fitting to have Jarelle and Warren in a children's environment. With this in mind, they were now standing with screwed up faces in little Samantha Cooper's room, decorated with all manner of things that screamed "girl".

"I don't like pink," Jarelle said.

"Then don't look at it," Hannah said with a smile.

"But it's everywhere!"

Warren didn't seem to mind too much. In fact, he had spied Samantha's various toys and began to reclaim them as his own. Suddenly, the perky doll that was designed for all sorts of shopping jaunts became something of an adventurer, fighting off her ascot-wearing suitor and establishing her fuchsia dream house as a fort.

"Can't I go get my console?"

"Not now, Jay. Tonight we just need to… stay here."

"But why?"

"Because… we need to."

"But *why*?"

"Because we need to," Warren said, not even looking up from his new doll army.

Hannah knelt down and held Jarelle by the shoulders. She could see that his frustration was turning into something darker, but didn't want to tell him all about the horrors that were unfolding outside. Instead, she thought of something, and placed him upon the bed.

"You know your dad?" she said.

"Course I know my dad," Jarelle said. "He's in Heaven now."

Hannah held back her emotion and kept her smile firm.

"Did you know he was a hero?"

"Daddy was a hero?" Warren said, rushing over to listen in as well.

"Oh yeah, a big hero. He did all sorts of things."

"Like what?"

In truth, Hannah didn't know what Greg did. But she did have an idea of what Perry and Stewart did. And what William and Charles Barrett did. And Heather Stanley.

And most of all, The Colonel. She had a very good idea about what he did.

So she told Jarelle and Warren how their late father, Greg, had fought monsters. How he had searched the land for them, learning all about them, and then either taming them to live alongside boys and girls like them, or defeating them if they were bad. Hannah told them how their dad was a warrior, who was smart as well as strong. How he was someone who never gave up, laughed in the face of danger, and always cared about the everyday folk.

Most of all, he did all this because he loved them, his family. He loved their mother, Hannah, and he loved his two boys. He made sure that the creatures in their closet were chased away, and the monsters under the bed were crushed. Hannah told them that Greg knew all of their fears, all of the things that made them scared, and battled against them every day to keep them safe.

"And now," she said, feeling it all well up inside her, "he keeps us safe from Heaven. Using his new powers."

"Like what?" Warren said.

"Lasers. And telekinesis."

"Telly what?" Jarelle said.

"It's that show I told you about," Warren said.

"No it isn't."

A brief shoving match ensued between the two, and instead of admonishing them, Hannah laughed.

"Boys, all I need you to remember is whatever bad things there are, whatever scares you or makes you feel tiny, there are people like your dad out there fighting them."

"And dad was the best at fighting them?"

Hannah smiled widely, a tear trickling down her cheek.

"Yeah, he was. The very best."

Jarelle and Warren seemed pleased with this story, and the latter told his brother to come join him at his new army base. There, the blonde haired dolly was now armed with a handbag claymore, with her multicultural allies ready in their bright pink car to tackle all sorts of evil.

In that moment, everything seemed alright.

But Hannah knew that these days, those moments didn't last.

Especially when she heard Heather scream downstairs.

Charles was the one to tell Hannah what had happened.

Once Rich's body was brutally pushed through the choke point of the hole, The Colonel continued his controlled descent. It would later be learnt that the cable that held him was unspooled using a control handled by The Colonel, meaning he neither fell down the hole with speed, nor took the slow approach as Rich first did. Using this, The Colonel gave himself enough slack to get through the tight walls of the hole, and through the iris at the end.

Much like Rich had told them all on his journey down the hole, it was The Colonel's feet that first kicked into the emptiness of the cavern. With his extra rope, The Colonel slipped through the walls of the hole and popped out of the other end.

There had been a pause through his communications with Heather, before he described what he saw.

It was indeed a gigantic cavern, and the sheer scale of it would make a person's head hurt. The Colonel couldn't help but feel that a person such as Rich would be blinded by what he saw, rather than be aware of what such a space represented.

Because while it was stupidly large, it was also quite improbable. One of the first things that you learn is that the Earth isn't hollow, and such an internal expanse goes against the ideas of various mantles and asthenosphere that make up the planet. At this depth, given how deep The Colonel estimated the cavern was, you'd expect some sign of the partially molten asthenosphere.

And yet, all he reported back was that he saw nothing but dark.

Except, that wasn't entirely true.

It took a moment of personal sanity for The Colonel to continue to describe his surroundings. Heather knew it before he spoke, feeling the tremor in his tone and the loss of grit in his words. The Colonel's words became cold, almost blank, and it was only a prompting by Heather that encouraged him to speak more openly.

Above him, where the aperture of the hole looked back at him, were walls covered in what first looked like small stalactites. When they began to flinch and feel the air around them, The Colonel knew it wasn't rock. He poked the wall and found it to be an organic, soft layer, of which the tendrils that hung from them reacted accordingly. Soon enough, the rod that The Colonel used to test the area went the way of Ronnie's finger, and was swiftly disposed of before it melted The Colonel's hand as well.

It was what was below him that was of most interest. Unlike Rich, The Colonel had a special torch as part of his equipment, one that had far much more illumination power. This meant, when he shone it below where he hung, he saw the surface more clearly than Rich had.

From the speakers of the laptop, those above ground listened as The Colonel described what looked like salt dunes, rippling waves of off-white crust that at first looked strange, but suggested it was still a form of mineral layer.

That was until it moved.

The ripples shimmered, and the dunes ripped through the light of The Colonel's torch at such a speed it hurt his eyes. At points, The Colonel noted pits within the silt-like surface, oozing a liquid that he couldn't identify.

And then, The Colonel saw what Rich saw.

The blood-red rivers.

The endless ocean of white.

And the central pupil of a colossal eye.

Above ground, there were no words. The air went still, and everyone felt their muscles clench and their nerves shimmer in anticipation. After decades of seeing such things on a far too constant basis, The Colonel didn't fall to the same hysterical insanity that struck Rich Davis. He didn't scream, he didn't cry, but instead simply told the facts as he saw them. There was something in the cavern with him, and that something was of a size that was inconceivable.

And now it was looking up at him. At least, that's how it felt to The Colonel. To this creature, he'd be no bigger than a miniscule scrap of dust floating upon a person's eye. But human beings didn't have thousands of tendrils lining their own cocoons, feeling at the cable that held The Colonel and wrapping themselves around it.

This is when The Colonel made his decision.

In all honesty, it shouldn't have surprised anyone.

Over the speaker of the laptop, he reminded Heather of his love for her. Charles told Hannah that The Colonel – James Stanley – had spoken such poetry, such a display of emotion, that in his honour he refused to spoil by remembering it incorrectly. Instead, the words had left Heather in solemn tears, and those present with empty hearts. The Colonel showed no fear, no desire to resist his fate, and instead told them all quite simply what his plan was.

"I'm cutting loose," he said.

And with the sound of a click, the cable whirled back up through the hole, and The Colonel fell into whatever called the centre of their planet home.

Heather's scream was actually a mild reaction, in Hannah's opinion.

Nobody considers the end. Not really.

This was what Hannah was hearing in the people around her. All fantasies of a post-apocalyptic wasteland, or a world left littered with sin after the Rapture. In truth, people wake up every day, go about their business, and don't consider the fact that the end can suddenly occur without warning.

This is what the likes of Perry did. This is what they prepared for. While August saw all the various paths that fate could take, Perry and the others around Hannah instead only saw one. They were blessed without the anarchy of an infinite level of realities, but cursed by the fact that their own destiny was, perhaps, already predetermined. Their story was told, their narrative carved out thanks to choices that they themselves never made.

It wasn't like the movies that Hannah had watched. It wasn't like the stories she'd tell the boys. By the time that August had informed Perry and Stewart that their world was past saving, there was little to do but wait. Unfair, maybe, but inevitable.

Like Harwood and Phelps had said.

"There must be something we can do," Hannah said, appealing to anyone who would listen to her. Perry and Stewart remained silent. William collapsed into a chair, wiping his face with resignation. Charles was the only one who remained on brand, finding the Cooper's cache of alcohol and pouring large glasses to share amongst those present.

Heather just left. She got up from her chair, walked past them all, and walked out the front door. The breeze that pierced the inside of the house was cold and thin. While the door was open, Hannah saw the HP workers waiting to film what was going to happen, even if they didn't know what that was.

In truth, none of them knew.

At this stage, only Hannah would dare try to flail against fate.

"Can we… destroy it?"

"Do you even know what *it* is?" Stewart said, clearly not in the mood for hope.

"Oh, leave her alone, Stewie," Charles said, passing her a large glass of unidentified alcohol. "She doesn't know any better."

"How about fuck you, Charles?"

Charles just shrugged. There was no point to offence.

"You can't all just sit there. Not now."

"Hannah," Perry said, looking out the window with dull eyes. "There's nothing else to do."

"Mum?"

To Hannah's dismay, Jarelle and Warren had decided to investigate what was going on. The two young boys looked around the room to see a lot of depressed adults, damned with the knowledge of what was to occur. It would scare them, if Hannah would allow it.

And she would be damned if she'd do that.

"You remember the monsters?" she said.

"The ones that daddy defeated?" Warren said.

"Exactly! Well, we're trying to figure out how to beat this one. Daddy had an idea, and we need to believe that he can tell us."

When both boys looked up to the sky for a response from their father, Hannah felt her heart skip. She knew this wasn't a time for emotion, though, and kept her cool.

"What do we think, boys? How would your dad defeat a monster?"

"Um, blow it up?" Jarelle said.

Charles scoffed, but Hannah took no heed. Instead, she prompted her sons onward.

"What if they were down a big hole?"

"There's a monster down the hole?"

"Mummy…"

"Don't be scared, boys. Be brave, like your dad would want."

The two boys looked at each other, and nodded in agreement. Greg had always made sure they were strong of spirit; he knew that was something they got from Hannah and made sure to nurture it. Right now, it would prove to be valuable.

"If we can't blow it up…?"

"Tell it to go away?" Warren said.

"I don't think it can hear us, buddy."

Warren considered this, and then looked over at the laptop.

"What about the old man?"

Hannah was confused.

"Can't he talk to them?"

"Warren…"

Before Hannah could fumble with the fact The Colonel was gone, Warren walked over to the laptop and sat himself up on where Heather had been. Jarelle wasn't convinced by his younger brother's skills, but Warren ignored him and leaned in.

"Hello, Mr Stanley?"

Hannah looked around. Every adult there looked drained.

"Mr Stanley, are you there?"

"You need to speak up, Warren."

Hannah's mind was scrambled. Thoughts were piling on top of each other, turning it all into white noise.

All of that cleared instantly when she heard it.

"Boy?"

The Colonel was alive.

The disbelief of all those present was only balanced by the casual way in which Jarelle and Warren Suggs spoke to their elderly neighbour.

"Mr Stanley, it's Warren Suggs here."

The Colonel just laughed.

"Can you do something for us?"

There was silence until The Colonel spoke.

"What?"

"Can you tell the monster to go away?"

"It can't go away, Warren, it's down in the hole," Jarelle said.

"Well, maybe he can tell it to be nice to us?"

Hannah couldn't believe what she was seeing. While everyone else, cursed with a mind made of logic and fact, the innocence of two children decided to see things another way.

One that could just work.

"I'm afraid I'm not near its ears," The Colonel said. He sounded in pain, with the subtle sound of swift movement around him.

The boys thought about this. "Where are you?"

"I'm on its eye."

This seemed to strike an idea in Warren.

"Then go to its brain! If you talk to its brain, it'll hear faster."

"What are you talking about, idiot?" Jarelle said.

"Daddy told us that when you speak in someone's ear, it goes to their brain. So if you talk to their brain, they'll hear faster."

"Their brain doesn't have ears."

"It's a monster, Jarelle, they can have anything."

Charles burst out laughing, swigging back his drink.

William sat there, gawping in disbelief.

Hannah was just proud.

While the boys bickered over the physiology of a monster, she took over at the laptop. She could hear The Colonel chuckling to himself, grunting as the ocular ground he lay upon threw him about at speed.

"James?"

"Your lads are clever, Hannah," he said. "Where's Heather?"

The room went silent; the only noise being the constant chatter between the Suggs boys.

"I see. Probably best."

Perry rushed over and leant into the speaker. "Stanley, are you OK?"

"I've fallen into the eye of this thing, agent."

"Understood, but…"

"But nothing. You know what? One moment…"

There was the sound of a gunshot, and then a giant rush of air. The Colonel grunted in pain before roaring out a cry. The sound of rumbling echoed through the speaker, and Hannah joined the others listening in waiting for The Colonel to speak again.

A moment later, the swish of ground was silent and a soft moan came from The Colonel.

"James?"

"Your lads are clever…"

"Thanks, you said…"

"The brain. If I can get to the brain…"

Cogs turned fast and wild amongst those present. Everyone cottoned on to the same idea that The Colonel was considering. If he could get to the creature's brain, then maybe he could do something to it that would stop it. Or tame it. Or at least something.

"I'm inside the head," The Colonel said, sounding weak. "If I find the brain…"

He laughed. The sound of a gun cocking echoed against organic walls.

"Kill the brain, kill the beast."

"Is that even possible?" Hannah said.

"Anything is possible, Suggs. Just ask your boys."

She looked over and saw Jarelle and Warren looking back, full of curiosity and excitement over the adventure unfolding. To them, this was just another action story with heroes and monsters.

The human aspect wasn't even a real consideration.

Things went quiet. Nobody moved as they waited for The Colonel to speak. After a few minutes, he said his last words.

"Time to die."

After this, everyone topside just heard his headset crumble over the laptop.

At first, nothing happened.

A state of catatonia washed over those within the Cooper household. They all remained in place – adult and children alike – and waited in silence for something to happen.

A few minutes passed, and still nothing did. But they remained stuck in place, refusing to say a word, as if any action on their part would bring about the end of the world.

In the past, Hannah would have considered something like this absurd. To her, the whole Butterfly Effect was just a curious thing to talk about at parties.

But after everything that had happened in Anton Court, after all the bizarre occurrences and weird strangers entering their lives...

Well, she firmly believed that one movement out of place would damn them all.

In the end, it was the bland tone of a mobile phone alert that broke the silence.

It belonged to Perry. She retrieved her phone, as did Stewart. As did William. As did Charles. It turned out, as one phone pinged, so did the others. All with the same message.

Something was happening.

Anton Court was minor in the grand scheme of things. It was a gated community, sold as an exclusive enclave for families and the like to make their home away from the hustle and bustle of normality. It was expensive, yes, but people like the Stanleys, the Barretts, and even Hannah's partner Greg, could afford such a luxury.

Because their employers - people like Perry, Stewart, and the strange August - could afford to pay it for them.

But the reality was that now, Anton Court was part of a larger picture. It was a key point in a large web organised by people like Harwood and

Phelps, the H and P behind HP Properties. It was where a hole was to appear, or a vent if you will. It was to be a centrepiece to be contained and utilised however they wished, outside the bureaucracy of the authorities.

And across the globe, these lands that they had bought, that they had protected as their own, finally began to bring about what they awaited.

These big things, these huge events happening worldwide, made the likes of Perry, Stewart, and the Barretts panic. It made them run about and search for a solution, something to do. Any ease they had with the end vanished once it was coming, and instead a survival instinct kicked in.

This was the reaction of those open to the big picture.

But to Hannah Suggs and her boys, Anton Court was their focus. It was their home, where they had decided to make their life. For a short while, they had, and then it was shunted violently away from the path they hoped for. A lover and a father were taken, and they were left with Anton Court.

Then they had the hole - the curious, bizarre, and alien gap in the ground. A geological invader to their cosy existence.

One that now began to speak more violently to them all.

It started with a rumble, as it did everywhere. A small tremor that caused the ground to judder and wave. Things weren't thrown about, but instead waddled across shelves and carpets. People remained in place, but any motion they did make was emphasised due to the quakes.

Then, the world began to explode.

The crashing noise was deafening, and the boys immediately clasped onto their mother. Hannah fell to her knees, holding Jarelle and Warren close, as the smashing of everything burst around them. The tremors turned into an earthquake, the ground now throwing everything upon the surface in a rage.

There were screams, but they simply drowned in the chaos that unfolded with staccato frequency. Things exploded, fires burst into life, and the hole vomited.

It was a pillar of sandy, yellow liquid, which burst from the hole with such ferocity it barely had space to spill onto the Earth itself, instead creating a jelly-like pillar into the emptiness of the sky above. Not all of it spewed into space; thin flecks splattered upon the ground, melting tarmac and turning anything organic into small, blue fires. Norris and the other HP people present, making sure their camera captured everything, found themselves struck with a torrent of this bile. It stripped Norris straight through, burning flesh clean off and disintegrating bone in a vertical line. Another splatter hit the new caretaker on the back of the head, and he fell to the ground to expose the hollow wound that fizzed there.

Hannah thought she heard prayers. She had no idea who was saying them. She could barely hear the cries of her children. She tried to reassure them, but instead a constant deep drone ripped through her ears. She closed her eyes tight and thought about what August had told her about other realities, other times just like this.

In another world, another Anton Court, everything was fine. They were having tea and toast, and everyone was happy.

But this was not that world. In this world, the ground cracked and punched away chunks. In this world, people ran and panicked and cried. Here, Hannah and her boys didn't laugh and eat and have a good time, they clung to one another, terrified.

"It's going to be OK," Hannah said.

The hole turned into a crater outside, the acidic torrent finally running dry.

"It's going to be OK."

Charles and William sat together, drinking direct from bottles. A fissure in the foundations below created a sinkhole, and they fell together.

"It's going to be OK."

Stewart was consumed by a fire, unable to put out something that wasn't created by any known minerals.

"It's going to be OK."

Perry watched as the first claws crept from the hole, spider-like in their speed and erratic movement. When the body of what these bony appendages belonged to appeared, she prayed to whatever gods were listening.

"It's going to be OK."

Hannah held Jarelle and Warren tight, and in the blinding white of her mind, saw Greg looking back at her.

"It's going to be O…"

In another world...

Everything is perfect...

Everyone is happy

During the Unbound campaign to get Deep Down There published, a couple more tales from the time the events in Anton Court occurred were told. Here they are for your pleasure.

I hope you enjoy.

OJ

We Wait

Well, I reckon it must have been about midday when the first car arrived, give or take an hour.

Me, Steve, and Bertie were sat outside the Station, waiting for the usual run of commuters cutting through Highway DT to get home quicker and needing some gas. The morning and the late afternoon are the usual busy times, so rest of the day we crack open some beers, and talk about life while looking at the sands roll about.

Anyway, this car arrives, and Bertie gets up to make a sale, only the car don't want no gas. Instead, it veers into the little parking lot where the drive-in used to be, and this young lady hops out as soon as the engine stops.

I'd say she was late 20s, maybe a little older. Dressed like she had come straight from a board meeting. But she ain't looking for business opportunities, no sir. She's looking for something else.

She must've looked in a panic for a minute or so, when Bertie called out to her. Asking if she was OK. She don't answer, and me & Steve share a chuckle at the whole thing.

Then, something clicks in her head, and she straight up pounds out to the middle of the desert. Must have run a good half-mile before stopping, looking, and then just standing there.

Bertie came back and thought it weird. So did we. That girl stood there stock still for a good while.

Until the other one arrived.

Same situation. Middle-aged guy pulls up, dumps his car, and runs out to where the young lady is. Now, this is where Steve is thinking some sort of shenanigans is going on. After all, if an older man and young woman are meeting in the desert, it usually means trouble's brewing.

Well, he just goes and joins her, and they link arms together.

Don't move an inch. Don't say a word. Just link arms, and stare out into the distance.

I tell you, at that point Bertie cracked open the good beer.

We must've watched for a good hour or two as two more cars arrived, and a couple more random folk go and join the girl and the guy. They arrive, link arms, and then stand there.

I think Steve said it best when he muttered, "now that's some weird shit".

But yeah, you knew about those four. The one you're wondering about came about 20 minutes later. Not just the lone car, but another trailing behind it. This one grinds itself in with a trail of dust, and the death of the engine. The one following looked like it was trying to block it in, but the driver wasn't planning on going anywhere. They were straight out, and already running by the time the fella got out his vehicle.

Turns out, the woman in the car he was following was his sister, and he had been trailing her since she left suddenly. You could tell he was plum worried, as he screamed and shouted at her as she joined the other 4, linked her arms in, and let them all create a perfect circle.

Now, this fella – the brother – he's not a happy chappy. He's screaming at her, trying to pull her away, do anything he can. Bertie, in his helpful manner, tries to go assist the fella, but you know what happened then? Absolutely insane now I think of it.

This other girl turns up. Little teenager she was. She comes out of nowhere and throws herself at this brother. She's scratching and clawing, and it took all of Bertie's strength to pull him away from her.

And then? She just sat there, watching Bertie and this fella.

He joins us, and tells us his name is Greg. Sister is Josie. Says how they were in hospital with their Mother when Josie gets this blank stare and leaves. Greg, being all pissed about this, tries to follow, and then their little chase began.

Course, Steve being all curious, asks him why she was coming here and joining the little circle cult out there. And you know what he said she said?

Of course you do. It's become their little mantra.

"We wait."

Well, sir, at that point he wasn't the only one who needed a beverage.

Bertie then goes up to them. Sees this little firebrand watching him as he walks toward the circle of folk. He has a quiet word as we keep an eye from the Station, and wait to see if Little Miss Claw-Happy attacks. But no, she just sits there, and Bertie comes back.

Says they said the same thing to him as they did to ol' Greg.

"We wait."

Steve wants to know what they're waiting for, but there's no answer to that one at the time. No, we just tried to look after this Greg fella, give him some booze to steady his nerves, and sit there while more people walk on the scene, and sit guarding the five in the circle.

Must have been a good dozen before you folks showed up.

I didn't even notice the chopper when you mentioned it. Guess we got caught up in the hoopla of this weirdness. Your cars come along – and you sure as Hell don't want gas – and you get out and do your thing.

Your buddy – Godson, was it? Well he's a sort. Like he was born out of a 90s action film. All shades and swagger. He was the one that pissed Greg off. Young man with that stress doesn't need wisecracks as answers. He's just freaking out about his little sister, and your man tells him to "cool off" with us elders.

Frankly, I would've been charmed if I'd given a hoot.

While you and your other buddies check out the circle, Godson gives us the questions. The answers I've told you above. Greg, though, he ain't playing nicely with this Agent. He's asking all sorts of questions.

"Who are you?"

"What's wrong with her?"

"Why are they doing that?"

Your boy Godson? He just tells him.

"Government."

"Mass hysteria."

"Mass hysteria."

I've been in wars; I've ain't ever seen mass hysteria where you all stand around in a nice little circle. Especially repeating the same damn thing to every person who asks what you're doing.

"We wait."

I mean, we were happy to supply you folks with beers and supplies. That Dawes sure likes his pretzels, I tell you that. Even saying you'd compensate for closing the road and killing ol' Bertie's business for the day – even week – was nice enough.

But don't try to sass an old hound. You'll probably get more bite than you expected.

I get it. I've worked with folk like you before. Was an incident in 'Nam where cool men in black suits come along and tell us there's "nothing to see here". So I get it. I also appreciate the sentiment when it came to letting us keep our ground. An old man has nothing but his place to stand, y'know?

That said, by God you could've given the young fella, Greg, a break. I know he tried a couple more times to pull lil' Josie away, and I know he got a few bruises from the strangers protecting them for it. But Godson telling him he will "pop a hole in his head"? That's a bit far for my tastes.

Right now, it's close to midnight, and apart from a few more of your finest – as well as a few more loons looking to protect the circle – ain't nothing more been done. Your man Godson tells us about this "greater good", but don't tell us what it is.

And if you guys aren't telling us jack, then we're just hearing the same song from those over there.

"We wait."

For what, is my question. Because no matter what your fancy technology says, there ain't nothing out there but sand and dust.

If you can see some holes down there, it's nothing but critters.

Localised entirely in that little circle of theirs.

So, you know, I guess that is a little weird.

Guess we gotta do what they say.

We wait.

The first thing that told them to land was the panic in the guards' movements.

The second thing was when they revealed they were armed. Or at least one was, and not too shy about showing it.

Not that this bothered Willard or Maine. They'd had guns shoved in their faces many times before. This unique skill was probably why they had been assigned to go check out this little bastion hiding on the Emerald Isle. The document they had been provided with said that some Russians had made their home there, courtesy of a group named Gostinitsa Cartography. A company so mysterious, there was nothing more to them than a name.

And a little hut on Emerald Isle, of course.

The pilot landed the helicopter a few miles from their intended destination, and the two agents pulled their coats up to prepare for the cold. While they did so the Russians, who weren't pleased about their presence, came running toward them, shouting in their native tongue.

"They don't seem happy, do they?" Willard said.

"Would you?" Maine replied. The two shared a smirk that they had shared on many occasions before, and jumped out.

By now, the Russians' approach had slowed, and both agents could get a proper look at their new friends. Their faces – hidden behind some well-crafted beards – didn't suggest any abject fury toward their presence, more panic. Like this was not what they had signed up for.

Of course, both Willard and Maine knew this, and knew to use it to their advantage.

"It's all good, eh?" Willard said, arms in the air and a smile on his face. There were a few good feet still standing between the two parties, and for now that would be fine.

The unarmed Russian shouted back.

"Well, I'm afraid that's not going to happen."

While Maine didn't speak Russian, Willard did. The fact that he refused to speak it back just showed why he had climbed so high in the ranks. You don't get to the higher echelons of their agency by not being an arsehole.

More Russian shouting followed, as well as a lowering of the arms from Willard. He told the two men that they meant no harm, and they were just here on business.

The unarmed Russian questioned this, and Willard was happy to answer.

"The hole."

Suddenly, the armed Russian decided to make his presence known. A rifle settled on his shoulder, and aimed straight at Willard. Maine thought about returning the sentiment via the pistol that was tucked away in her jacket, but thought better of it once Willard starting to play ball rather than wind up.

"<You know what I mean? >" He said, finally putting those Russian language lessons to good use.

"<You must leave. Now! >" The armed Russian said, still holding his rifle in shaky hands.

"<I'm afraid that isn't going to happen, friend. What is going to happen is that you're going to lower that gun, and show us the hole. >"

"<They'll kill us, >" the unarmed Russian said, looking desperately between both groups.

"<Not if we can help it, >" Willard said, turning to Maine with a smile.

"<They will! They have our families. Our friends. They know too much. >"

"<Do they know what's down the hole? >"

Willard paused for effect.

"<Because we do. >"

Only the bracing wind of the Arctic made noise for the next few seconds, before panic gave way to defeat, and the armed Russian became the second unarmed Russian.

"You certainly have a way with people," Maine said.

"Well, you just have to speak their language."

Now the formalities were over with, Willard & Maine followed the two Russians as they walked toward their hut. It was barely habitable, but a quick peek told Maine that it just about kept the two men in water and comfort. What they really wanted to know about was a mile or so to the Northeast.

Once they got close enough, the Russians stopped, and Willard & Maine made the rest of the walk unaccompanied.

"Bingo," Willard said.

Before the two agents, in stark contrast to the whiteness of the Isle's natural ground, was a deep, dark hole exactly five and a half feet in diameter.

Just like the report said.

The memo came through a few hours later, and Shen grabbed it to take directly to Adams. Speed wasn't quite of the essence, but within the Bureau it was nice to keep things prompt.

In Adams's office, Shen laid down the report, and waited for a response.

"Contained?"

"Yes, sir. Any threats have been neutralised, and the site is now secure."

"That's what I like to hear, Ash," Adams said, rising from his chair and moving to a map on the wall. There, he plucked out a red flag, and replaced it with a green one.

There was a silence as Adams looked over the map, and Shen remained standing on the other side of his desk. The agent looked from side to side, wondering if his superior would turn round, and after a brief moment of shuffling, decided a verbal cue would have to do.

One cough later, and Shen had Adams's attention once more.

"Something else?"

"More than likely. A development in England."

Adams's curiosity piqued a little more.

"Reports have come back saying a new company of interest has launched. Called HP Properties."

"And the HP stands for…"

Shen just smiled.

"Thought you'd like to look over their brochure," Shen said, producing a glossy leaflet from his jacket, and placing it on top of the Arctic file.

Adams had a brief look over the cover, seeing all manner of bright greens and blues, as well as the usual stock model family gazing lovingly at their new home.

"Anton Court… heh. Nice name."

"Shall we…"

"Of course, Ash. Ol' HP is always worth a little surveillance."

Shen understood, and left Adams' office to begin work on the new development. The lead agent turned back to his map, and looked over the multitude of flags on display.

The Arctic flag was the fourth green one.

There was a Hell of a lot of red.